MAGICIAN'S HOARD

MYSTERIOUS CHARM: BOOK 3

CELIA LAKE

Cover design by Augusta Scarlett.

 Created with Vellum

ALSO BY CELIA LAKE

The Mysterious Charm Series
Outcrossing
Goblin Fruit
Magician's Hoard
Wards of the Roses
In The Cards
On The Bias
Seven Sisters

Find a complete list of all my books at celialake.com/books.

Sign up for my newsletter to be the first to hear about future books and learn about fascinating bits of research. Happy reading!

ABOUT MAGICIAN'S HOARD

There are secrets hiding in the ground.

Pross thought she had a straightforward research question to solve. A widowed bookseller, she took on the project to help make ends meet. All she has to do is help her client uncover the truth about the stories of a hidden hoard on the family estate in Norfolk. But the Research Society she knew through her late husband has changed, and the only person who will speak to her is Ibis Ward. And he's rather prickly about it.

Ibis knows his colleagues don't care for him. He's both too foreign (if only half-Egyptian) and entirely too competent for their comfort. He spends his time using his fluency with hieroglyphs, his archaeological skills, and his gifts for magic to translate and describe newly uncovered items brought to London from Egypt.

Despite himself, Ibis is intrigued when Pross asks for his help. When it becomes clear there's more at stake than a single Roman hoard, he finds himself trusting her more than he's trusted anyone in years.

Share the archaeological adventure with Pross and Ibis in 1926 as they are drawn into a web of magic, mystery, and those who use magic and power for their own ends.

ONE

JANUARY 1926, LONDON

This was an uncomfortable chair in an unwelcoming office, and the day did not promise to improve. Pross had been sitting patiently for twenty minutes. Despite her careful choice to wear one of her better dresses and a becoming hat, and carrying a formal notecase, she felt decidedly out of place.

Once, the city had been familiar to her, when she and Octavian were apprentices and then newlyweds. They'd had the comfortable flat, near the woman who'd taught her the fine books trade. She remembered the narrow streets in Southwark, the hidden village of magical folk tucked in among the other spaces of London. Then they'd had the years in Trellech, where magic flowed more freely and more comfortably, before moving back to the New Forest, near his parents in Salisbury.

It was the contrast, perhaps, that got her. For all the New Forest wasn't her original home, it was warm and welcoming. She had friends there; she knew the way the road sounded outside her window, and the angle of the sun in the winter and summer. She could feel people near but not too close and step outside her door whenever she wanted a little company.

London felt different, distant and cold, everyone hurrying to their own particular goal, without noticing what was going on around them. She had come up last night, stayed in a small inn by the Southwark portal, and walked up this morning, to stretch her legs. She suspected some of that was the weather, as mid-January was not the best season anywhere in the British Isles, but it was not just the weather.

London had changed a great deal in the years she had been gone. Pross was not sure how much of it was the War, how much was the endless march of technology, how much was a shift she could not measure. Some of it might be that she had, irrevocably, changed, after losing Octavian, making the places they might once have visited together raw and unfamiliar. And yet, she did not particularly want to make a concerted study of the question, going round to each place in turn.

What she felt did not matter. Here was where the Research Society was, just west of the great British Library and the British Museum, just south of University College London, and the Petrie collection. In the midst of the minds of the ancient city, as it were, not the banking or business or even the arts districts. She should feel at home here, or at least a welcome guest, and she did not. .

Octavian had always spoken of the Research Society with such pleasure. He had spoken of warmth, of being in the presence of amazing collections, of turning the corner into fascinating conversations everywhere you went. He had talked about being surrounded by history, of each corner revealing some new detail, some new facet to learn. Of course, the Society had moved since then, due to the

War and the shifts of spaces. But in contrast to his stories and descriptions, this place was barren.

It was a Georgian home, perhaps two or three merged, it was hard to tell from what she had seen so far. But where Octavian had described wall hangings, prints, and copies of historical works, the walls were blank, minimally white-washed. The few bookshelves she could see were half full, and with what seemed to her experienced eye to be poor quality work, at that. They were the kind of thing an avid reader picked up at estate sales for a pittance, or for that one chapter or a handful of mentions. A book of some use, but not the kind of thing one would highlight if one had better, certainly not befitting the reputation of the Society.

Worse, they had left her for some time, after an abrupt welcome by the man on duty. A rather pinched-looking older man peered at her over his glasses, and muttered under his breath. She had introduced herself politely. "I am Proserpina Gates, my late husband Octavian was a former fellow and spoke well of the Society. I wrote, ten days ago, to make an appointment with whatever research fellow would be best suited to a question concerning a document, and I was told to come today."

The man had snorted, fumbling his pen, before he took down her details. A document concerning a probable Roman object, based on certain information. Finally, he came to the end of whatever he was writing, and said brusquely, "Have a seat, ma'am. I will see if one of the fellows is available."

It had been thirty minutes at least now. She had thought writing for an appointment would mean someone would be waiting, and she'd had a short note confirming her appoint-ment time, but apparently not.

Eventually, she heard the older man stumping back, the

slight thump of a cane on wood floors. "Mr Ward is in. He will see you." The older man was sitting down, looking disgruntled.

"Is that who my appointment is with?"

"That is who is here, miss." That stung. She was a widow with a child about to go off to school herself, not a schoolgirl.

"But my appointment." Now she was whining. That wouldn't do either.

"Mr Ward is the only researcher available." He glanced down at a calendar. "The next possible appointment would be late March, with..." He flipped a page or two. "Anyone else."

Pross knew when she was defeated.

"Which way, please?"

"Here." He reached behind him, to a set of hooks. "It will open the stairs for your visit. Third floor, right at the top of the stairs, last door on the left."

She blinked and said "Sir." before she went back to gather her portfolio.

"Stairs." The man jerked his thumb at the main stairs. "Don't wander. It isn't..." He paused, considering his words. "Advisable."

Pross blinked once more. "Of course." She gathered her skirt in one hand to keep it from catching on the portfolio.

Why it had to be three flights up, she did not understand, and in what seemed the furthest possible office from the entrance. At least the directions were easy enough to follow, if not the most pleasant in good shoes. Finally, she came to a small door at the end of the hall. The plaque outside said "I. Ward" or possibly "T. Ward." The imprint was not entirely clear.

She lifted her hand and knocked.

"Who is it?" The voice inside was a man's, and he sounded annoyed.

"Pross - Proserpina Gates. I had an appointment?" Her voice rose at the end and she cursed herself for sounding so insecure. It would do her no good.

"Not with me." The voice was abrupt.

"The man at the desk sent me here, Mr Ward." It was the name on the door, it was presumably the name that went with the voice.

She thought she heard a sigh from inside, and then a "Door's open." She undid the latch, an old-fashioned piece of metal that offered next to no security, and pushed the door open.

The man behind the desk was surely younger than she was, and at first she thought he was tan, before she realised it was his natural skin tone. He was not as dark as Octavian had been, but it still went with dark hair on the longer side than fashion encouraged at the moment. He had an English last name, and yet that was not at all what she might have expected to go with it. On second glance, she still thought he was younger than she was, but not by too much. Early thirties, maybe. He wore a rather faded tweed suit, the mark of an academic who didn't fuss about his clothing.

He wore glasses, and was peering over them at her, making a disgruntled tsking sound with his tongue. Either he wasn't aware he was doing it, or he didn't care about offending her.

When he spoke, it became even more clear that his background was not purely British, by the rhythm of his voice, and the clipped accent. Egyptian, perhaps, or Indian. His posture and how he'd laid out his desk suggested a background in the colonial government, she'd seen it often enough with her father's colleagues.

"I'm Ward. Someone sent you up?"

"My name is Proserpina Gates. I wrote to make an appointment, I got a confirmation card."

He waved a hand. "What is it regarding?"

"I would like to consult the Society about a particular document. I am advising someone local to me about materials that have been in the family for many years. They relate to some sort of discovery. I suspect Roman, but I am not sure yet what era, or of other details."

The man - Ward - waved his hand. "I don't do Roman. Well, not outside of Egypt. Speak to someone else."

TWO

LONDON

"There is no one else. Apparently." Pross was getting somewhat annoyed. Scratch that, rather annoyed. Her voice was sharper than she meant, but still.

The man looked up at her, blinked, and then said, "I have no idea where they all are." She stood, and waited, and, with obvious reluctance, he relented. "Let me have a look. I expect it's not my skills you need. Miss."

He had settled into a tightly contained, proper mode with her, she recognised the tone of someone dealing with a momentary bother who could be handled by following procedure. Father's staff had shown her how that worked many a time.

"Mrs Gates. My late husband Octavian was a Fellow here, following his apprenticeship, for a few years. I am afraid most of the people he knew are gone now." She did not let herself to dwell on that, or on his more unfair loss, but she could not let the misinformation continue.

The man inclined his head. "I'm Ward. Ibis Ward. Fellow in Egyptian artefacts. Reviewing the Petrie collection for items of magical interest and concern." And then, as if his manners caught up with his tongue, "My condolences, ma'am."

"Thank you. It's not recent, though. Half a dozen years." Her voice came out clipped and tight. It wasn't Ward's fault. Trying again, she said, "I thought the Petrie collection was donated before the War? Octavian took me to some event, related to it."

His face shifted in a momentary rise of some strong emotion, then it settled back into that impassable politeness. "Donated before the War, ma'am, but not fully evaluated. There are over eighty thousand items in the collection. The professor is most zealous in his guardianship. But we can work around the edges, and I have been able to study a number of objects under the cover of translation efforts."

Pross found the idea quite distracting. "So he does not know you are evaluating them for magic."

"No, ma'am."

"And you read hieroglyphics?"

"Hieroglyphs is the proper term, ma'am, for the letters, hieroglyphic refers to the system of writing. Noun and adjective forms." He was very precise. "I also read Demotic script, ma'am, and a handful of other languages."

She raised an eyebrow. "I presume also Latin?"

"Some." He wouldn't lie about that, she presumed.

"My document, then." She reached for the portfolio, unfastening it and drawing out the folder inside, card stock protecting the sheets of letters. "The first two are the relevant ones."

Ward shifted a few things on his desk to the side then took the folder, opened it, and adjusted his glasses to read. He was reading the Latin with some fluency, the way his eyes shifted across the page.

"Mmm. And you came across this how?"

"I'm assisting someone in the New Forest, they had materials from other family up in Norfolk. I'm helping go through the papers."

"Why did you pay attention to this?"

She shook her head. "I'm a bookseller, mostly. Not a scholar, like my husband. My apprenticeship trained me to pay attention to those little moments of intuition. Those are what make a bookstore. How to spot what people are looking for, when to approach them, what you choose for small talk. I like the challenge, but it's not scholarship."

Ward looked up at her, sharply, and she met his eyes without flinching. Octavian's peers had teased or ignored her for so long, it didn't really hurt anymore. Not like it had, once. She held his gaze until he looked back down.

"You said Norfolk. That is where the family's from?"

"My client's father's mother. They still have the property, but no one's lived there in ages, except for a caretaker. Run down, she said, no modern amenities, even if modern means Victorian."

This made Ward laugh, the first human sign he'd shown her. "People like their comforts. And the paper?"

"With a batch of others, about items found when building a new barn, and someone's maps of the land and a description." She tapped the folder by the sheets. "The top one is about the landscape, and a description of a barrow. The second one has some legends, about people saying there was treasure there."

That got a wave. "People say that all over Albion."

"Here, it might be true. Or more true. But I can't figure out - there are half a dozen places it could be, it's a large property. And some of the landmarks have changed."

"Since the twelve hundreds, I hope they have." He

leaned down to peer at notes in the margins and murmured something under his breath.

"I believe those are a dialect of Middle English. I make the copy fifteenth century, maybe early sixteenth, I'm waiting for some tests on the ink to come back. As far as the language, I'm consulting someone who reads it better than I do later this week." Pross felt she should be clear about what she knew already.

"What did you want from the Society, then? You seem to have most of it covered." He looked up at her as if he was expecting something.

She made a frustrated noise. "I know what it says, but I don't know how to interpret it. I'm not an archaeologist, I'm not a materia specialist, I'm not a linguist. There could be a puzzle or a warning or a... I don't know. Probably not a curse. I read too many novels."

This won her another fleeting smile. "Curses are less common than they're rumoured, yes." Something in him was lighter now, had there been something in the documents she'd missed? He was definitely more interested than before. "Do you want an archaeologist, a linguist, or a materia specialist?"

She gestured at the pages. "I would like to find out about the..." She stopped, tried again. "Those describe some sort of notable object. My client would like to know what it is, the history, how much of the stories are real." She paused, and then had to admit, "Of course, she's got old houses, all of which have a creaky roof or a leaky one. It's not like money would be a bad thing. But the knowing, more."

Pross knew she sounded rather defensive.

Ward nodded. "And what is your role in this?"

"To see it through. Solve as much of the puzzle as can be solved, which might not be a lot. Advise my client if there is anything worth pursuing." Pross thought she sounded prissy, but it was true enough. "Gather the information and make sense of it, as much as is possible."

Ward leaned back in his chair, unbending that far, at least, and took his time before he answered.

"We are supposed to do a certain amount of consulting work." He was drawing it out, for some reason.

"Sir, I know that the fellows of the Society are meant to consult, but not the scope." She folded her hands in her lap, trying to hide her uncertainty.

He gestures. "We can do an interview like this, direct you to sources. We might undertake portions of the research ourselves. In rare cases, we might do field work. Most of those I've met here don't care for it." He paused then tapped the folder. "I rather miss it."

"You have previous experience?"

"In Egypt," he said. "A little here. I am less familiar with the techniques for wet ground, I admit." He let his finger trace in the air along a few lines.

Pross waited.

"My Latin is - not well suited to this task. I've enough for magical work, but not for nuanced translation. You'd have to see to that. But I believe I could consult about areas to investigate outside of that. Advise on approaches. And I have no little experience evaluating objects from digs, or the arranging an excavation itself." He gestured at a stack of papers on the end of a bookshelf, rather haphazard.

"Your fee?"

He tapped his fingers, named a figure. "Flat fee. I find I'm curious." He settled back in his chair, watching her response.

Pross thought through it. Her client had given permission to go up to a certain amount. This was perhaps ten hours of consulting time. "If it takes more time?"

"No extra charge."

"If it takes less?"

"I'll refund the additional at standard rates."

"Why?" She would be blunt.

"There are hints, in the text, that intrigue me. Can you make a copy? May I make a copy?"

She produced another folder from the portfolio. "A copy in a clean hand, a working translation, the words that are unclear because of wear or connotation noted in different colours of ink."

He flipped through the pages. "You are very attentive."

Pross nodded, nervous again. "I am thorough."

"You must not be resident in London."

"No. My bookshop is in True Eyeworth, in the New Forest. There's no portal close, I'm afraid, that's public."

"Are you able to come up again in a fortnight?"

She did the mental calcuation and nodded. "I can arrange that, if we make arrangements for a Friday or Monday." Cammie could join her in London for the week-end, one of her visits home from tutoring.

They settled the details, and she left the copies with him, retreating with her portfolio, his business card, and a profound uncertainty about what had just taken place.

THREE

LONDON

"Hathor's horns, but they're so... British."

Ibis more or less refrained from slamming the cabinet door. It would do no good.

He heard a rumbling from the other room. "Trouble in paradise?" Ibis turned, looking over his shoulder out of the narrow galley kitchen, and scowled at his flatmate.

"Jonas."

That got a broad grin, and a "Come on, mister grumpy. Have a drink. Tell me about it."

Jonas was a medical student, of all things. From a magical family, of course, but he wanted to learn medicine he could back up with science. He'd come from a prosperous enough black family in America. People still made assumptions, he said, but in London they were easier to live with. Or at least different.

Judging by the half-drunk beer in his hand, easy was not on the menu today.

Ibis pushed away from the counter. "Let me take you round the pub."

Jonas shook his head. "Not fit for public. But if you want to go bring food home?" He let his voice trail off.

Ibis nodded. "My turn." he agreed. It was often his turn, between Jonas being on his feet all day, more people fussing at him, and also having a smaller stipend. He slipped his jacket on and went out, returning fifteen minutes later with meals from their favourite local. Which is to say, the sole one within five blocks that served them promptly and without difficulty.

They set the food out on the tiny table in the sitting room, as local custom would encourage, and poured fresh beer. Ibis murmured his prayers, stood to put a spoonful in front of each of the two carved stone images on his shrine near the west window, then sat down. They both spent several minutes in silent appreciation of the food.

"Your day?"

Ibis shrugged. "Curious and then frustrating."

"Your colleagues?"

Ibis nodded. "You know we're supposed to take it turn and turn to deal with consultations, and I was handed the duty all through the holidays. I was not supposed to be on the rota again for another three weeks. And yet, ten o'clock this morning, there's this woman knocking on my door. From what I got later, I was the only one even in the building, other than Davis."

"The front desk man."

Ibis nodded.

"So what did this woman want?"

"She had some documents. She's a bookseller, she was assisting someone local to her, going through old papers. There's a hint of a lost treasure, you can imagine the foolishness."

"Did she go on about the gold and the treasure and the fine things?"

Ibis shook his head, sharply. "No. Actually." It came out harsher than he meant.

Jonas blinked. "Not at all?"

"No. I mean, she mentioned the money wouldn't be a bad thing, if there were money. For her client, or I presume for her. But she was more interested in the history."

"And you liked that." Jonas let the drawl slip into his voice, and Ibis snorted.

"Intrigued." He waved a hand. "She's a widow."

"And you know that how?" Jonas was amused.

"Her husband was a Fellow, back when. Before the War."

"She doesn't sound so horrible."

Ibis shook his head. "She wasn't the problem. She was," he considered how best to put it.. "Mrs Gates was very matter of fact. Sensible. Nice change."

Jonas laughed. "What was the problem, then?"

"She left copies of the materials with me, tidily organised. And I locked them up, and when my theoretical colleagues arrived, I went round to ask them."

"I gather that didn't go as well?"

Ibis shook his head. "Varney was her usual rude self. Not interested in anything outside Londinium, thank you kindly, possibly Bath. Pitcher was actually nasty, questioning why anyone would want to speak to me, rather than his usual disdain. Bathurst - well, that was forty minutes I won't get back of him rambling on about buttons."

"It's a button month, then."

"The lead figurines are almost tolerable. By comparison."

"Simpson?"

Ibis grimaced. "Twenty minutes of lecturing about when he was a Fellow, he had a lot more to show for it. When he was a Fellow, he wasn't having to hide what he was doing from the esteemed professor who donated the collection."

"And you only make much progress when said esteemed professor is in Egypt."

"Yes. Professor Murray isn't nearly as difficult, when she's in town, fortunately, well, not about that. But the various others." He shook his head. "Which means I've some time free at the moment, alas."

"Aimtree?"

"Not in evidence, but when is he ever, unless it is much to his advantage." Which meant people who might fund his projects, or invite him to the kind of parties that had him straggling to the Society offices well past luncheon the next day.

"Same old, then?"

"You?"

"Same old, too. Wearing more today than some. Other people getting preferment, told about opportunities, that sort of thing."

"You don't actually want a Harley Street practice."

"Well, no." Jonas stretched. "But I'd like to feel like it was mine to turn down. Given the chance."

Ibis snorted. "What do you want, then?"

"To live between the worlds and make my own way, treating the people who need a touch of that to heal." Ibis tilted his head at the way it came out, solid and certain.

Jonas got up to clear the plates, clapping him on the shoulder. "You look startled."

"The way you put that." He went quiet, thinking, while

Jonas cleared the table, and brought back another beer for them to split, pouring it into each glass.

"It's true enough. Look, tell me more about your widow." It came out easily, fluidly, like a shift in harmonies in one of the latest jazz improvisations.

"Not mine." It was instant. Only then Ibis wondered if Jonas were deliberately deflecting.

"You are not usually this interested in people who talk to you at work."

That, Ibis had to grant, was quite true. He tapped his fingers on the table. "There was something about her. No, not like that."

"Like what?" Jonas was leaning back, broadly amused.

"I tried to turn her away, originally. She didn't have an appointment with me. But she was persistent."

"That is not generally a thing you appreciate."

"She wasn't rude about it. She just wouldn't go away. So I told her to come in, and she explained her problem, and she didn't tell me how to solve it. She knew..." Ibis considered. "I like that she was honest about what she didn't know. She said she wasn't an archaeologist, or a materia specialist, or a linguist."

"And you are all three."

"I've spent years honing all three crafts, yes. Not that my languages are much use to her, I'm quite sure her Latin is better than mine, and her Middle English certainly is. I always feel like there are piles of marbles in the middle of the vowels."

Jonas snorted. "Much better than I am, anyway, on all of it. That's your British classical education for you."

Ibis laughed. "Well, you aren't the one working as a Fellow of the Society, so it works out." He continued "Anyway, she intrigued me."

"You like digging in the dirt, you mean."

"It would be a good excuse, if there's anything in the story. And right now, I'm stuck working from my notes, and not likely to get back into the collection for a good month or two at best."

"So a little distraction might be the thing?"

Ibis shrugged. "It has some promising puzzles, the pieces I've looked at in depth. There might well be something there. If there isn't, we should figure it out fairly quickly. The site's in Norfolk, so not too bad to get to."

"And the woman? Is she likely to be difficult?"

Ibis shrugged. "Nicely dressed, though she lives in the New Forest, so I assume she can manage the sort of trudging around the countryside required." He half-closed his eyes. "Sensible hair, dressy shoes, not much in the way of cosmetics. Older, maybe forty, maybe even forty-five. You know I'm bad with how old women are. She wears her wedding ring though she mentioned her husband died a half-dozen years ago."

Jonas snorted. "That's very precise. What did you make of her, then?"

"She was nervous, coming to us. Oh, she put a good face on, looked entirely respectable. She spoke well though I'd have expected that. Schola, I assume, but I didn't see a ring or anything to make me sure. And her notes were well organised and managed."

"Intelligent and she didn't... did she talk down to you? I suspect she didn't, or you wouldn't be considering this."

"She didn't. She didn't comment on me as I am, at all. Just the information at hand." Which was rare enough.

Jonas sighed. "Forty's old for me."

"You are only twenty-five. Also, as I said, she's still wearing her wedding ring. That suggests she's not interested in finding another husband, even one as intelligent as you are." Ibis kept his voice light, since they both knew there are all sorts of reasons a respectable widow might not be interested in someone like Jonas. Class, country, race.

"Children?" Jonas was irrepressible.

"She didn't say. She had to think for a minute when I suggested meeting in two weeks. She said a Friday or Monday would be easier, but she didn't need to consult with anyone else. I assume if there is a child or caretaking or something, there are days she is not responsible for it."

"Not Jewish or at least not observant. Nor Muslim?" That had a more questioning tone.

"She seemed very much your ordinary English sort of woman. Whatever that is, she was it. You do go on, Jonas."

"If you're going to work with her, I would like an image of her in my head to attach your grumbles to."

Ibis snorted and said, "Don't you have things you're supposed to memorise? I've a journal to read." He was entirely done with this line of thought now.

FOUR

LONDON

"Ward, old man." The tone was false-hearted, Ibis could hear that at once. He was coming back from his lunchtime walk. The habit was normally safe enough, since most of the others in the Society favoured long lunches at one club or another. He couldn't help a glancat his watch. Only half-twelve. This was deliberate, then.

He turned on the front stairs, his hand on the door latch, and nodded. "Aimtree."

They were about an age, but Ibis was always struck by how young Aimtree looked. Public records suggested he'd had an easy War, easier than most, which might explain some of it. Ibis did not have the connections to sort out if that was chance or someone's preferment. Probably preferment, given the man now.

He came and went as if research were something that could fit into a few bored minutes in the mid-afternoon. He favoured long lunches and drinks at the club where he could talk to the right people. There was a vague and perpetual stink of the too-easy path about him. Ibis's father would have dismissed him as 'unsporting' at first meeting.

A man with such a charmed life, in the prime of his thirties, should do something other than being a fellow at the Society. The Society itself was prestigious, but the fellowships had historically gone to people who needed the stipend. Or those who needed access to a particular collection, or who preferred office and library research above all else.

It was the second for Ibis, though the stipend didn't hurt.

"I heard you had a caller, yesterday."

"I did." There was no point lying about things Aimtree already knew, and besides, he had asked around the Society after Mrs Gates left.

"That's rather out of your league, old man? I thought you didn't touch anything north of the Nile Delta. Which is relevant enough to some people, I suppose." He dismissed the current work being done in Egypt with a wave of his hand. Ibis caught sight of the cufflinks, a sudden flash of an almost coppery colour out of keeping with his other clothing. Aimtree normally preferred gold. Visible gold.

"I was the one able to see to the question, yesterday." He paused to consider why the man might be bothering him, then said, "Not really your thing is it either, I'd have thought?"

What Aimtree's thing was, well, that was a mystery. He preferred research that kept him in London, talking to fashionable, wealthy people, and no hint of getting his hands dirty, or the rest of him. He was now, Ibis believed, engaged in cataloguing a series of jewelled shoe buckles from the 1770s.

Ibis supposed that all things were better catalogued and

labelled, but he would personally have put jewelled shoe buckles further down the priority list. Much further down. Aimtree's answer was unlikely to be useful. But if ibis paid close enough attention he might figure out what the man was after.

Aimtree shrugged, in the current fashionably dismissive mode, which suited him well. "Oh, Varney mentioned it was some family, holdings up north, and I do know rather a lot of people, old chap, I'm sure I might lend a hand." Something seemed to shift in him, a faint shimmer of something perhaps magical, that faded from Ibis's vision as rapidly as it had appeared.

Ibis had the instinctive desire to raise all his defences, from the unfamiliar strangeness of the vision and the urge to protect his project. He called on what both his parents had taught him, the balanced disarming forthright politeness that often worked in these situations, or at least made it impossible to accuse him of duplicity or rudeness. "Oh, I'm afraid I'm not sure of the location. I've only a few rudimentary copies of texts to look at."

"You don't say. Do tell me more about your visitor, perhaps I can guess at where."

It was the last thing Ibis wanted, he knew he needed to keep Aimtree well away from this. And from Mrs Gates. If the man managed to slither his way into the project there would be no removing him, and even if he could be trusted to respect her proficiency, he certainly would not be competent to address the archaeology himself. And Ibis rather suspected Aimtree was the sort to have wandering hands.

"The client was a bookseller," he said. "Out in Hampshire or Wiltshire, out in that area. Those are in the same area, aren't they?" Never mind that his English geography was rather better than Aimtree's, since he acknowledged there were things outside of London. He knew there was even rather a lot of land north of Yorkshire and Cumbria.

"No address?"

"She didn't give one - she's a widow, I'm sure she didn't want to confide her particulars to a stranger."

"And how'd she come into the information, then? In a book?"

Ibis shrugged. "She didn't detail that process, just said she'd come across them, was looking into them. Her own curiosity, perhaps. I didn't press her."

"You said you had a copy?"

It was quite unusual for Aimtree to be pressing this much on anything that involved anything like effort. There must be some reason, some compelling reason, even if Ibis had no idea what it was. He'd suspect Lord Sisley's hand, but this seemed a small thing for the head of the Research Society to meddle in. "It's in Middle English - not your forte, old man, unless you've been hiding your skills under a bushel?"

Aimtree shrugged. "Oh, I might have picked up a thing or two. Mother English, of course, we get bits of it in school, even when we're little, that I'd not expect you to know."

Ibis took a deep breath. "I learned English the same way I learned my other mother tongue." he says, easily. "Father was quite thorough in his stories and in his tutoring, but this is a dialect I've not seen much. She said she knew someone who might do better with it."

Aimtree pursed his lips. "No map, then?"

"Nothing so informative. A few references in letters she'd copied out, or papers of some sort. She didn't even give me the context, you know how shoddy I think that." Mind, he had no doubt she knew exactly what the context was.

He'd have to ask her, next time, if he could see what she'd found all together.

The question had Ibis distracted for a moment, thinking about how to approach this puzzle like he would an archaeological dig. How could one apply that intuitive sense of something hidden under the sand, waiting to be rediscovered? Could one even have that sense for manuscripts or words on the page? She had said that was what had brought her to the Society.

It meant he missed Aimtree's next comment and had to say "Pardon?"

There was a decided note of irritation in the other man's voice. "I said..." There it was, the gloss slipping away. "You really ought to hand it off to someone better suited." There was that flash again, like the glint of scales of a snake about to strike, or the bubbles in the river that hinted at predators under the surface.

Ibis shrugged. "I've a thing or two, quite within my scope, I said I'd do for her. I'll hand it back to her, or find her a suitable specialist, whichever is needed." He waited a beat and said, "I do know the proper process. There's a contact at the British Library who might consult, he's known me since my Schola days."

Aimtree tsked disapprovingly and then said, "Well, if you end up with egg on your face, that's your fault."

Ibis took a moment to judge how to respond, and then said cheerily, "So kind of you to take an interest. Do have a good day, Aimtree, I've a few things I want to work on this afternoon."

He climbed the stairs up to his office briskly, hoping that Aimtree wouldn't venture the extra flights past his own first floor door. Fortunately, the man's laziness had come back and he did not pursue his uncharacteristic interest further.

FIVE

TRUE EYEWORTH, A VILLAGE IN THE NEW FOREST

Pross couldn't figure out why she felt out of sorts. For a wonder, she had a morning free in her flat with her best friend, before the afternoon Market Day.

"So, tell me about your visit to London." Ferry stretched. "We've time. My little ones are with the nurse-maid, I don't need to be home until at least four, and we don't need to set up for market just yet. You've been ducking the question since you got back."

Pross shrugged. "It was a little baffling."

"Baffling how?"

"Some of it was how London's changed."

"You spent quite a lot of time there, when you were younger, right?" Ferry sounded rather wistful.

"When Octavian was apprenticing and a fellow of the society, and when I was apprenticing, and a few years after. Though mostly south of the river, for me."

"Why didn't you stay on?"

"The War. He didn't want me in the city, in case, well, cities are awfully good targets. And we didn't have any family near there. Well, he didn't." Pross settled down across the table from Ferry, putting the plate of scones in the middle where they could both enjoy them.

"So you went up the night before."

"Stayed in an inn near the portal. There's a little magical village tucked into the middle of the city, and then a few other clusters in other places. Southwark, that's where I apprenticed. One up near the Royal Society, in Bedford Square. Something at the edge of Spitalfields though I've never been to that one."

"You believe that thing they told us in school, about why cities have less magic?"

"How having more people changes the flows of the natural magic and makes it hard to do complex work? I think I do. It feels different there, certainly. I think..." Pross paused, searching for the words. "I don't think that there's less magic, but I think it's a different kind. Some people thrive in it, but a lot of people maybe don't."

Ferry considered that, then nodded. "I like that explanation better than all the non-magical people draining it off. That just seemed... awful, somehow."

Pross snorted. "You should have been in Owl, the way you insist on logic."

Ferry grinned and reached for a scone. "So. Your visit. You said Octavian had been a fellow there."

"He had. They've moved spaces since then, and I was only in the old space for parties and such. But this felt different. Very empty. Not much on the walls, the books on the shelves I saw were... strictly second rate."

Ferry raised an eyebrow. "They must be, for you to say that. You've never met a book you didn't want to cuddle."

Pross flushed. "It's not their fault, poor dears. But the sort of thing that someone wrote because they had funding for it. Or they needed the publication credits, or, well, some

of them were the project of two decades of someone's obsession, too. Those are always interesting as concepts even if
the prose is awful."

"So things didn't look like you'd expected. What about
the visit?"

"I'd written ahead, you were here when I sent it off.
And someone had sent back a little printed card confirming
the visit. But when I got there, there was a porter or
someone who was very abrupt. And he said there was only
one person there who would take a visitor."

"That's queer."

"Rather, yes. All the way up at the top of the building - I
think they must be a couple of Georgian houses opened up
to each other off one staircase. And he was on the third
floor, up in the attics, what would have been servant's
rooms, all the way down at the end."

"Not somewhere you put your best and brightest."

"Oh, he was excellent." Pross bristled and Ferry put her
hand up with a murmured apology.

"Tell me about him?" Ferry offered after a moment's
silence.

"Striking, both appearance and manner." Pross said,
after a moment. "Anglo-Egyptian, I'm fairly sure, given his
name - Ibis Ward - and his speciality, which is Egyptian
artefacts."

Ferry chewed on her lip for a moment as if trying to
remember something. "I can look him up when I get home?"

"Oh, would you? You've got the books."

"If I don't, I can certainly rummage in Ytene's library. It
would make Carillon and Lizzie quite happy, they say I
don't take advantage enough."

"You've been a trifle busy," Pross said, smiling.

"Two children, all the things to finish my apprenticeship. And a husband whose job running the stables has had him out on foal watch most nights for the past two months." Ferry shook her head. "Which is why getting today free was such a thing."

"You are thriving, and you know it."

"Deliriously." Ferry agreed, grinning. "But that doesn't mean I don't like time to hear about what's up with my best friend."

Pross shook her head and went back to the story. "There was something about how he set out his desk, his things, and his voice, that made me think of the Colonial Service."

"Like your father."

Pross nodded. "Younger, of course. I think Mr Ward a few years younger than I am. Mid thirties, give or take a year or two."

"Is that the ordinary sort of age for a fellow of the society?"

"A bit old, actually. Most people his age would be provisionary or full members. But the War disrupted a lot, and the membership has quite a lot of required publication and research."

Ferry considered that, then gestured for Pross to go on.

"I explained the project, and he asked some sensible questions, after clarifying that this was not at all his area of expertise. I liked that." Pross let her voice trail off.

Ferry leaned forward. "What did you like about it, then?"

"Oh, most of the scholars I've met, they want to play oneupmanship games, prove they know more than you. More than half. It was refreshing to meet someone so up front about his limits."

"How did he treat you, otherwise?" Ferry was working on something, Pross could tell, but not what it was.

"Abruptly, to start, but politely. Sort of gruff. A little grumpy, but not at me, more at... the interruption and assumptions of the porter?"

"Huh."

Pross shrugged. "Anyway, he asked what I wanted, and I said to sort out the puzzle. And I wasn't sure if I needed an archaeologist, or a linguist or a materia specialist, but I needed skills I didn't have."

"What did he do?"

"He thought for a little and then said he'd be glad to consult. That they have a fair amount of scope in what they did. Quite reasonable terms, my client's already agreed."

Ferry blinked. "That suggests he's interested, then. Or at least not solely concerned with money?" She sounded a little baffled.

"Your husband rubs off on you, Ferry, love."

Ferry shrugged. "He spent so long without money, even now things are steady. That's not something wears off that easily. It's not like I don't have my challenges as a wife sometimes. Him needing to know we've plenty set aside is a much better thing to manage than many others I can think of."

"That's truth."

"Your Mr Ward."

"Not mine. But I'm going up, Thursday next. Mrs Billings agreed to come mind the shop again. I'll do a little checking for stock, meet with Mr Ward on the Friday, and then Cammie's coming for a visit."

"And you can show her London."

"She's been asking for ages, and I wasn't..."

"You weren't sure about the memories."

"Exactly. When - it's easier here, somehow, the place we came to when we knew what we were to each other. But there's so many memories in London, of us getting to know each other, and figuring out how to make the marriage work."

"At least it worked out for you." Ferry's voice turned a little sour.

"Your parents didn't have any sense at all, trying to set up a match. Mine did. And Octavian's. Even if it meant we married before we'd spent more than a dozen days together."

Ferry shook her head. "How's Cammie doing? It's been ages since I saw her last, and you know she's not good at letters."

"Doing well in her tutoring and looking forward to Schola. Her tutor says she'll be fine when she gets there, she's mostly polishing language skills right now."

"And the rest of her group?"

"Still enjoying them, being with people her age, and there weren't that many here, with your former charges also off for tutoring." Pross tapped her fingers on the table. "Octavian was so insistent about how going to Schola knowing people made such a difference. I could have taken it or left it, everyone I was tutored with ended up in different houses and specialities."

"But you were tutored, well. One of the Colonial Services places."

Pross nodded. "Most of them went into Boar or Bear." She waved her hand, with the memory of it. "Not like me. Not bad people, but different."

"What do you guess about Cammie?"

Pross shrugged. "I'm honestly not sure. There are ways she reminds me of some of Octavian's friends in Fox, the unconscious certainty that comes with the best of them? And she's got an Owl's intellectual curiosity, I like to think.

But it's - it's not like they tell us how they make the choices. And it affects so many other things. Who people spend time with. Some of what they learn."

"Every house has its merits. And for most people I know, it's worked out well." She grinned. "Mind, I'm envious of all the indexing and cataloguing magics Owl seems to teach."

"They don't work for things, and you know it's your threads you want to keep track of." Pross grinned. Ferry's weaving was getting better and better, and she'd be earning quite a name for herself shortly. Likely enough to resolve the household money issues and more.

"But I could write that down!"

Pross laughed, and said "Come on, finish your scone, and we can go down and you can rummage in my new acquisitions. I do owe your Lord Carillon a thank you for letting me use the portal at Ytene for the trips. You'll have a better sense what would amuse him than I do."

"For that, you really ought to get Lizzie down here, but I'll do my best to fill in."

SIX

LONDON

Ibis spent the next two weeks researching, mostly on the challenge Mrs Gates had presented to him. He was startled to find that Tuesday's post brought him a tidy packet with additional notes and materials. She was much more prompt than most researchers, and in clearer handwriting than was the norm as well.

He waited impatiently for her arrival on Friday, the 29th. They had set the time for nine in the morning, hoping there would be no one to disturb them or bother her on the way in. He anticipated they might be a few hours, and perhaps after that he could escort her to visit the British Museum, just across the square.

The knock on the door was quite welcome, and he called out "Who is it?"

"Proserpina Gates."

"Do come in." Ibis stood this time, as she pushed the door open, and shook out her umbrella. It was apparently still raining outside.

"I'm not too early?"

"Not at all. I've been here since eight, I like the quiet. Do, please, set your wet things here by the vent, so they can dry. And I have tea here, but of course, quite separate from the worktable. Do you need refreshment now?" He felt like this was all quite stilted.

She shook her head. "Thank you, no." Pross looked around, then smiled. "This is quite cosy, I hadn't really noticed last time. A comfortable workspace."

Ibis hated the cramped quarters, all the implied insults tucked into the angled ceiling and small space. He had tidied up, to find enough space to store the Petrie notes until he could return to them. It made the place look a little less crowded, but it didn't make it spacious.

But now he looked at the space the way she might see it, he could see there were homey touches. The lamp on the round table in the corner where he had tea. He'd found it in a second-hand shop near the flat, but the blue-green glow was like faience. The few familiar things on his desk, the small marble baboon statue, and his pen case. He kept a vase with a few fresh flowers and a dish of clear water on the bookshelf next to it, a shrine away from home. They added their own touch of beauty.

He startled, realising he'd been quiet too long. "Thank you for sending the notes along so quickly, they were quite helpful."

"I have the translations, I just got them yesterday, or I'd have sent them ahead." Pross glanced around. "I should sit here?" She gestured at the chair facing his, across his scarred desk.

"Please." He had an impulse to push the chair in for her and chalked it up to the shifts in formality, how she shifted from friendliness to business. Or perhaps his social skills had wasted, in his months spent working on translation in isolation.

Once they were settled, he said, "Where would you like to begin?"

"If you'd open with what you've sorted out so far, then perhaps I could fill in as I have new information?"

"Of course. I took a bit of time to review known material about Roman sites in the area in question. There are only hints, references without clear locations, in most cases, unfortunately. I think a site visit will be necessary, but I was able to create lists of relevant landmarks and geological features."

"Have you studied geology, then?" Her voice was curious, he thought, not the usual disbelief he so often heard.

He didn't answer for a moment, trying to decide, and she continued. "I'm sorry, I didn't mean to - you mentioned you had a range of skills, and it might be good if we were to share our lists a bit more. See where we overlap and where we don't? Or is that presuming too much?"

The idea made him smile for just a moment. "You are not telling me I cannot possibly know my field, so you are one up on a number of people I talk to already, Mrs Gates."

"If we're working together, do call me Pross."

"That feels quite improper, ma'am. You are my client." Something about her first name made him feel uncomfortable, for all he couldn't actually name why.

She tilted her head to the side, pondering him. "I would prefer to think of us as peers. I have skills you do not. You have skills I do not. We need each other to unravel the puzzle, or two people who match in..." She paused. "In duality, is that the proper term?"

He could feel his eyes widen, before he could suppress his reaction, put a proper English repression in place. He looked away instead, feigning a cough. He had not expected that from her, an understanding of the way he naturally looked at the world.

When he looked back, she was watching him with a kind of ageless patience that reminded him of the great carvings and statues that would outwait eternity.

"May I ask, you were educated at Schola?"

She nodded. "You?"

He could not tell whether she meant it as an honest question, or could not believe he'd have attended. He watched, looking for some sign, and she sat there, patient and unyielding. Eventually, he had to answer her, or things would become even more awkward than they already were.

"I as well. Though I don't think we overlapped?"

She snorted. "Oh, it's easy enough to not recognise half the people there when you were. Different houses, different years. But if you were there when I was, you were not in the Owlery."

"No, ma-" He caught himself, yielded to her argument. "Pross."

She beamed at him and then considered. "I am not sure what house I would guess you were. I've been thinking about it - my daughter just passed her entrance exams, so she will have a house of her own next fall."

That gave him more information about her than he'd nosed out before. "Are you hoping for one in particular?"

"Her father was Fox. I'm Owl, as I said." She moved a little, and he could see the pendant hanging around her neck, the white stone catching the light. She returned to peering at him.

"Trying to decide what I am?" He meant it to come out differently than it did. As it was, it was almost teasing. He was not at all sure what to make of that betrayal of the words slipping out before he could catch them.

"Oh, yes. That's a fascinating puzzle. It always is, no one ever explains why people end up in which house."

"Some things are mysteries, and should perhaps stay so."

"I thought you liked solving mysteries?"

"I do, but I think also that if the process for assigning houses were well-known, people would subvert it to their own ends. Certain powers corrupt from within. And I am not sure that a better system exists."

"This one has worked for centuries, there is that."

"More or less, yes."

She seized at that. "You don't feel as if you entirely fit your house, then?"

He shrugged, minutely. "I do not..." That sentence led to dangerous places. "I do not feel entirely at home with British fauna, I suspect."

That got a nod. "You grew up elsewhere, then?" When he hesitated and did not speak, she added "My father is in the Colonial Service. I grew up in India - Calcutta and Shimla, if those mean anything to you - until they sent me for tutoring here."

He immediately nodded. "You understand some, then." he says. "How different it is. The weather, the climate, the land beneath your feet, what it feels like, not just how it looks, the smells, the food."

She lit up. "Oh, yes. There's nothing enough like a spice market here, not... the way it stretched on and on. The sounds, the music, the festivals." And then a face. "I do not miss the snakes, mind. Or the tigers and wild boars."

That made him laugh. "It was crocodiles and hippos, for me, besides the snakes."

"Crocodiles, I understand. But a hippopotamus?"

He waved a hand. "Most dangerous animal in Africa."

"Egypt, then." It was not really a question.

"Egypt. Alexandria, to be precise."

Pross considered this, and again, she gave nothing away in her silence.

SEVEN

LONDON

There was a long pause, before Pross shook her head and said "Egypt - oh, it's foolish of me, but I've found the stories fascinating. Except I'm quite sure the ones I can find in books miss a lot of important things. That kind of telling always does."

She found him blinking at her, startled by something. She kept doing that to him, and she wasn't entirely sure why. It was unsettling.

"Did you find that about India?" he finally asked.

"Oh, Merlin, yes," she said, laughing. "People read Kipling and think that's all they need to know. And Kipling gets some things right, but he is awful about others, and he can go from one to the other, sentence to sentence, with no sign of the switch if you don't know he's doing it."

That earned her a thoughtful expression instead of a baffled one, which she supposed she would count as progress.

"I would hate to think I had to give Kipling up entirely."

This made Pross thoughtful. "He - some of his attitudes are distressing," she said, slowly. "He is generally far better about the animals of India than the people. And he likes, well, last I heard - some men who did entirely awful things."

She spoke cautiously, all the scraps of commentary catching up with her. Low-voiced conversations when she was a child, and the passing hidden references in letters since. Her father had been carefully distancing himself from some disgraceful acts of the Colonial rule, as much as he could, but Dyer and O'Dwyer and the rest still had their quite vocal supporters.

Pross looked up to find Ibis watching her, with that same intent focus. "You aren't the usual sort who comes out of a Colonial Service family, are you?"

She bristled. "I don't think there's a usual sort. Besides, I've been in Albion since I was eleven, one of the Service tutoring households." She cut off further commentary there, for her memories were not good.

He must have caught something in her expression and murmured "Pardon. I shouldn't press." It had a hint of something more complicated, like he thought she had power to hurt him if he didn't apologise enough. Like her ayah back in India, apologising to her father for some minor problem, and yet terrified she would be thrown out of the house on the spot.

Pross took a long breath to settle herself, and offered, "I like *Puck of Pook's Hill* very much, I admit. The sense of history being connected. I read it to my daughter a lot."

Ibis nodded, and then said, after a moment, like she had finally won a concession, "I was in Seal. At Schola, I mean."

Pross looked up, not sure how to take this change of subject.

He gestured. "One prefect, when I was having trouble adjusting, said it's the house of the liminal space, of living between land and sea, and never quite fitting either. I've thought a lot about that, since."

Pross nodded and was quiet for a good half minute. He let the quiet be. She liked that about him. "That seems a good description for..." She gestures. "Young people, in general."

"And those of us from two cultures, the moreso."

He was including her in that. She wasn't sure what had inclined him to do so. She had to think about it for a moment, then said "You think I qualify, then? May I ask why? I'm as English as - well, for all the First Families pride themselves on purity of line, we're rather a mix here. Angles and Saxons and Normans and half a dozen other things." She felt her sentence and her sense had got into a confusion in the middle there and winced.

Ibis murmured, "You understand how other people live. Or at least you don't assume you know. That's a rare enough thing. Colonial Service, especially."

"You've not had an easy time with them?"

"I was one of them, for long enough. Not an easy time, no."

She leaned back, watching him, then said, cautiously, "Intelligence, in the War?" She wasn't sure what she expected in response, he was far too competent to let his feelings show here. Instead, he let his hand drift casually over a jar on his desk and spill it, upending a dozen small objects onto the bare desktop.

"No fair," she said, immediately. "You know what's in your cup." She permitted herself a brief glance, a bare five seconds, then recited the list. "Small white pebble, a bit of erasing rubber, three gold beads and one silver, not round because they bounced but didn't roll, a chip of faience, a stub of a pencil, and some small carved stone I didn't get a good enough look at, it fell behind the..." She peered at the corner of the desk. "Small carved baboon at the corner there."

He laughed at this, and she was startled by how much she liked the sound of him laughing, like something miraculous had opened. "And what did you do in the War, Mrs Gates?"

That earned him a grin, and an "I keep my secrets, sir," said in a tone she hoped would not close off the glorious openness of his smile.

"I would expect nothing less," he said, after a pause that had her worrying she'd pushed too far, nodding his head graciously.

"And you a gentleman," she replied. "Many would push, or insist they had a right to know."

He pursed his lips. "Does that even work?" He sounded baffled.

"They like to think it does. Too many of my husband's colleagues felt a woman existed solely as a foil to a man. They might value an intelligent woman for producing clever children, and for asking the right questions to allow the man's knowledge to shine."

"That sounds unpleasant." It slipped out of him before he could stop it, judging by how he looked sour as soon as he heard what he'd said.

It made her laugh. "Rather. My husband did not subscribe to that journal's style guide, as one might say. Thankfully."

Ibis nodded, then ventured, "You said he was a fellow here?"

"Eastern Europe. Hungary, mostly, the period between the Romans and the man who became Saint Stephen. He did rather a lot with some early history of the area, the sources relating to the blood oath of the seven tribes. Both the history and the magical theory rather than the two separately."

Ibis blinked. "That sounds quite unusual, ma-... Pross." And then he considered. "Your husband was Octavian Gates, then?"

Pross nodded. "Yes." She was a little cautious now.

"I came across one of his articles, two or three weeks ago. It was about analysing non-magical artwork to test the ritual magic techniques used in the event in question. A case study of a particular painting, I believe, but I'd have to look up the name. I found the arguments against it predictable but not at all sound."

Pross laughed. "Oh, I know the one you mean, and I agree. One should hope for a better quality of criticism, don't you think? Not that many people have the language skills to offer alternate interpretations, at least not writing in English."

He offered a faint smile. "I'm afraid Magyar is rather outside my language skills."

"Mine too, though I can order food and read enough of a sign to follow a map," Pross admitted.

That earned her a snort, and a "If you know a reason-able restaurant for such things in London, I would be glad to try the cuisine."

It was a rather personal comment, given his reserve so far, and she nodded. "I'll have to check my notes at home, but I'd be glad to send you what I know about."

With that, he coughed, and said, "I suppose we should turn our attention to our actual research for the moment?"

She laughed and agreed. "We were going to compare skills, weren't we, and then you were going to lay out the groundwork for me?"

Ibis nodded. "I am trained as a researcher, not an archaeologist, but I have been able to work on and assist at digs in Egypt. Never as the academic in charge, you understand."

"People not being able to see past their own noses, I assume?"

It was bluntly put, earning her another of those startled, baffled nods. "But I know the skills, and better than many with formal titles. And the other related skills, a general understanding of geology and surveying."

"And languages?"

"Fluent in English, French, literary and spoken Arabic in several dialects, competent for most purposes except specialised translation in German and Latin, and well-read when it comes to hieroglyphs and Demotic." He paused, then added, "I should in all honesty admit that my hieratic is not as good as it should be."

"The difference?"

"Hieroglyphs are the - pictures, the distinct characters. Demotic and hieratic are forms of writing them more quickly, not shorthand, but letters that are faster and easier to shape. Hieratic is used for priestly texts, Demotic for other kinds of text. Law. Administration. Business."

Pross considered this, and then offered her own list, rather than pressing him further. "A variety of forms of English, including Old English and half a dozen dialects of Middle English. Quite fluent in French and Latin, moderately so in German. And, as I said, enough Hungarian to order a meal."

It made him smile a little. "And your other skills?"

"Book research, mostly, though more of the form of finding information, the sources that might have it, than original research from primary sources."

He nodded, then said, "So, if I begin by discussing the Roman settlements of the area, and what kinds of things might be expected, we should be on solid enough ground if you ask me for explanations if you need to."

She solemnly nodded, and said, "I will ask if I lose my way, yes."

EIGHT

LITTLE BEAULIEU, A VILLAGE IN THE NEW FOREST

I bis was not at all certain this was a good idea.

His meeting with Pross had gone well, but by the time they were wrapping up, it was clear he would need answers to quite a variety of other questions before he could do much more.

Once they hit that point, he escorted Pross across the road to the British Museum. They had gone past the showy objects, the Rosetta Stone, the great statues, and into the smaller rooms with the more obscure items. He spent his lunch hour explaining things to her, enjoying how she acknowledged the great works, but found the smaller domestic ones of more interest.

She had promised to arrange a meeting with her client before he left her to enjoy her afternoon, and she had kept her word, promptly writing back to arrange the details.

So it was he stepped out of a portal at Little Beaulieu at about eleven in the morning, in a little wooded area behind a magical inn, bustling with trade. Someone minding a small herd of sheep called out, "Oy, out of the way, you, some of us has work to do, not dawdling."

The noises, the smells, the feel of the ground under his feet, they were so different from London it startled him, and then he was shaken by realising how it was like being back with his mother's people, in the village with the cousins, along the Nile. The land was different, the colour of the ground was different, the language was, but he knew how this worked.

He stepped smartly out of the way, making his way around to the front of the inn. Pross had said she'd meet him there, since they weren't quite sure when he'd be able to get through the portal. Her client was near the Beaulieu portal, though apparently they were rather further from the village Pross lived in.

He was quite relieved to see her seated at a table within easy sight of the door. "Here, we've time for an early lunch before we meet my client. She had business elsewhere this morning, she'll be about forty-five minutes."

Ibis settled down, a little uncertainly. "Do you recommend anything?"

"Are there things you don't eat?"

He wasn't entirely sure how to take that - some people assumed that because he was Egyptian, half-Egyptian, that there were many things he did or didn't do. But from her, it seemed a more general question. He half-remembered there were a number of people in India with such restrictions, maybe that was it.

"Depends on the food, but I admit most of the things I don't care for aren't likely to turn up in a British pub." And it was easy enough to avoid the peas cooked to mush, over-stewed meat, and so on.

"The shepherd's pie is quite good. Or the cottage pie if you don't care for lamb. We're near enough the ocean the fish and chips are quite fresh. Or they do a decent round of ham and cheese and pickle."

He considered, then put in an order for the fish and chips and a half pint, when the woman came around for their orders. Pross, he noted, ordered the shepherd's pie and a half pint herself.

"You've been here before?"

She nodded. "My client's about two miles north, she has a little pony cart. Toward the Eyeworth road."

"And that's where you are?"

Pross smiled. "Been researching me?"

"It was," he said, with some dignity, "In your appointment file."

That made her laugh. "Well, that's just making it easy." She paused, then said more carefully, "There's a room free tonight at the inn in True Eyeworth, just down from my bookshop. If you wanted to continue discussing a bit more in the morning. I don't know if you need to get back?"

"I thought you said the only portal was down here, or Salisbury? Isn't that rather roundabout?"

"There's an option for tomorrow - not a thing I'm permitted to discuss in public, but quite safe and quite efficient, I promise." She watched him, very attentive now. "Do you trust me that far?"

He nodded. "I brought a change of clothes, as you suggested. Though that's good practice whenever one might find oneself crawling around spaces with artefacts."

"It's not a tidy profession, is it?"

He had to smile at that. "No. And the parts that are the most tidy, well, I think they're also a bit sterile."

She considered that, and at that point the beer came, and they were mutually absorbed in tasting and comparing.

"Ale," he said, thoughtfully.

"Not your usual?"

He shook his head. "The place we usually go to runs more to porter and cider."

"You must live in London? We?" Her voice got cautious.

"I've a flatmate, a medical student. Magical family, but learning non-magical techniques at one of the hospitals in London."

"Were you friends before, or..." Her voice trailed off.

"Both men from backgrounds that made it hard to find people willing to live with us. He's a decade younger, but we get on well as flatmates. I travelled quite a bit when we started, so it helped to have someone in the place."

"Research?"

"The same project I'm still working on, yes." He paused, almost about to tell her about his sister, but perhaps no, that was too personal.

The food arrived then, sparing not need to make more conversation. She worked around to "It's just me at home at the moment. My daughter's at one of the tutoring halls, did I mention?"

He nodded. "You mentioned." And of course he'd remembered.

"She met me in London, the last time I saw you, for the Saturday and Sunday. We had a grand time. I took her back to some galleries, shared a few of your explanations. She thought the cosmetic palettes quite fascinating once I could explain why they were like that. And that little turquoise hedgehog cosmetic jar."

Ibis had to smile a little at that. "I'm glad, then. Not many people are interested in the smaller things. It was..." He had to search for a better word than 'nice'. "Refreshing to talk to someone who was." Then he paused and said, more carefully, "Hedgehogs are interesting creatures, aren't they?"

She looked at him for a moment, and then said. "They always rather struck me as liminal, too. Nocturnal, like owls, being different from the daytime animals. And the hedges. There's rather a rich folklore of hedges as a liminal space."

He considered, nodding without comment.

Pross continued. "I thought it rather unfair that hippotamus in the next case got more attention. Especially with what you'd said about how dangerous they are."

"A rather far away fear for most people there, I'd assume." Ibis shook his head, and then changed the subject. "What should I expect from today, then? Plan for?"

Pross shrugged, setting her plate aside She went over the materials they'd be reviewing. Then, more quietly, she said "Philly is - good hearted. But she's very loud and takes up a lot of space."

Ibis nodded, and settled into asking questions about that, and more background about the family. Pross clearly knew the details well, she was able to draw lines between the current family and the ones who had won those houses and lands in the first place. He asked a few clarifying questions, and relaxed into the amiable, professional conversation, for the fifteen or so minutes they had before they were interrupted.

"There you are!" Everyone could hear the hearty, boisterous voice, attached to a broadshouldered woman in tweeds who had just arrived. "And here's your expert, you said?" she added, as she made even more clear she was Pross's client by approaching their table.

"Ibis Ward, this is Amphillis Tipson. Philly, this is Ibis Ward."

She looked him up and down. "Ibis, is it?" she said,

rather skeptically, like she wasn't entirely sure, or did not approve.

"Formally Thutmose, ma'am, but I normally go by Ibis."

She sniffed, and Pross raised an eyebrow. Amphillis shrugged and said. "Boy's got the cart outside, we should be on our way, so you can have a few hours with the things. Did you make arrangements, Prossie?"

Pross winced, behind Philly's back, at the nickname, but nodded. "The carter is meeting us at the head of the drive at half-six."

"It'll be long dark by then."

"We're going straight up the main road, and it wasn't bad coming down." Pross's voice was even. "I've done this enough, Philly."

That earned another snort, and a "Your own head be it. You have enough to keep you warm, then?"

"Brought a case, yes." Pross had picked it up from where she'd kept it tucked by her feet.

Philly led them out to a pony cart loaded in the back with several crates of materials and another that had at least one chicken in it. "In you get. Sit right on top."

Ibis was a little startled. "With the chicken?"

"Chicken won't bite."

Ibis shook his head, and said, "Well, it's not a goose. I really would have to object to a goose."

Which made Philly burst out laughing. "Oh, not such a stick up your arse as might be, then."

Pross ducked her head, and he couldn't tell if she was smiling or horrified. Perhaps some of both.

The road to Philly's manor house was bumpy, the chickens complained each time they went over a rut, and Ibis's legs were aching from balancing by the time they pulled into a large house, about twenty minutes later.

"Got the things in the armaments room."

Ibis leaned over and said, "Armaments? Should I be worried?"

"Swords stuck on the wall, mostly, so not terribly. They're not Philly's preferred weapon. It's where the big vault is, where the papers and things live. The really important ones."

Ibis nodded, then said, "May I take your bag?"

"Oh, I can manage." Pross said promptly. "It's blankets, for going back up - we'll be in the cart about two hours. We're a bit northwest of Beaulieu now, going more north and west to True Eyeworth."

"Thoughtful," Ibis murmured.

"I have sandwiches, too. And flasks of hot tea."

That made him smile. "Practical, thank you."

And then Philly was there, noisily shooing them into a rather dire stone hall at one end of the house. "The table, there. Bags over there."

They obeyed, though Ibis noticed Pross was as bemused by the tone as he was. Once they were settled at the table, Philly brought over two large leather-bound books. "These are the documents. And Prossie said you would want a map of the Norfolk estate that's here." She gestured at the other end of the table. "It's old, but it's what we've got. Lots of old around here."

"Can you tell me what you hope for?"

"Well, to find the hoard, of course. You thick or something?" Philly was blinking at him. "I thought you said he was clever, Prossie."

"He's being clear about the para- about what the scope of the work is. I told you that. That's why I'm glad he's helping, he will do things I can't. Can you - give us a bit? We won't be any bother."

Philly hmphed and said, "Should see to the chickens."

"I'll come find you when we're ready. Or you come back. Just. We need a bit to look at things and sort it out."

That earned Pross another hmph, but Philly went bustling out.

"Pardon. She doesn't quite get how research goes. She thinks you should look at the thing and have it make sense. I pointed out if it were that simple, people would have found the hoard centuries ago."

"What did she say?"

"She went hmph." Pross giggled at that, her politeness finally cracking. "Um. Here. This is the one I started with. You might thumb through and see if there's anything else that looks relevant? Some of it's in Latin."

They spent the next two hours poring over the volumes. He read out a working translation, she wrote it down, then he'd go back and read out the Latin so they'd have that for a more thoughtful translation later. Tedious, but it gave him specific things to look for in the papers as they went.

Pross had paused to stretch when Philly came back. "Tea, I suppose? Were you finding anything?"

"A few hints." Ibis said, cautiously. "Do you know anything about an old - well? Cistern? Place with water?"

He was watching Philly's face closely right at that moment, and he saw her expression light up with something akin to smugness or satisfaction, before her face smoothed over. "Something like. They'd have needed one up there. Not on the map, then?"

"Not this one, no. There might be others." Ibis did his best to sound dubious.

"I can rummage, see if there's anything else."

Ibis nodded, and Philly left them to go on with it, and

Ibis offered to scribe while Pross read out the Old English texts. "You'll have to spell them, mind."

Pross nodded, and that kept them busy until it was time to get going in the cart. Ibis was about to say something, once they were tucked into the back of the cart with blankets with warming magics and flasks of piping hot tea and sandwiches, but Pross shook her head. "Sleep on the work, talk about it in the morning. I'll get you settled in the inn, it's been a long day."

NINE

TRUE EYEWORTH

Pross felt all the better for a night's rest. At nine, she walked down to the inn in a light chilly drizzle to meet Ibis, and found him finishing a rather expansive breakfast.

"Morning, George," she said, to the innkeeper. "Morning, Ibis. I thought we could bring your bag up to the bookshop, and you can leave from there."

He was a little wide-eyed, startled by something. In general, she thought, not specific or in the immediate past. She turned to settle up the bill with George, and then shooed her consulting researcher out into the street with his overnight case.

"Do you have a specific time you need to be back?"

He was looking around, his breath forming puffs in the wind and mist, watching people set up for market, some of the stalls with windbreaks, some people who'd just work from their shops. "No?" he said hesitantly.

"I thought we'd head out around one, then. Give us time for a good bit of work, and lunch. That would get you back to the London portal well before dark."

He nodded, still visibly distracted, and she settled in to walking quietly up to the end of the street, and the stairs to her shop. "Here, this way. The shop's closed Saturday mornings. Someone offered to open up this afternoon for me, so I can see you off. We can work down here. But honestly, upstairs is more comfortable and closer to the kettle?"

Ibis blinked at her. "Upstairs?"

"I have a flat upstairs. Unless - do you have..." She paused, waving a hand. "Octavian's family ran to odd geasa. One of his uncles couldn't be alone with unmarried women, even little girls or babies. Another one couldn't be in any room that was yellow. If there's some reason upstairs would be bad, I can bring things down?"

He shook his head, and she discovered he was smiling. He was struck again by the way she thought about things, checked to see if there was something that would make him uncomfortable. "Not a problem for me if you don't mind. And we have been alone together before."

"In the Research Society. I'm fairly sure that's not encouraged... no, actually, Octavian told me stories, of when everyone had had too much sherry. Or port. And closets."

This made Ibis blush, and stammer, "I didn't mean that."

Pross took a step back. "Oh, I'm teasing. Here, take off your cloak? We can hang it up here to dry. And you can leave your overnight bag here. And then through that back room, and up the stairs. I'll be right behind you."

He blinked at her owlishly for a moment, before he handed over his cloak, settled his working bag on his shoulder, and followed her instructions. She could hear the creak of the stairs as she took a moment to hang his cloak so it would warm up and then followed him.

She found him standing in the middle of the kitchen, apparently unsure what to do next. "The loo is through there, if you need it. And there's the table, or there's the two chairs, here."

"Is there one you prefer?"

"The blue one is usually mine, and the purple one is - well, it was Octavian's. Now it's Cammie's when she's home. So right now, yours. Do you want tea?"

Talking about Octavian was always complicated, how he wasn't here, and yet all the things that had been his, had been shaped by him, were. The furniture, the layout, the teas she kept in stock or didn't. Everything was affected by him, somehow.

Ibis settled cautiously in the purple chair, then reached into his bag, pulling out several items and the working notebook he'd used the day before. "Can I help?"

"You get your notes ready. I just need to steep the tea, had everything ready. There're scones for later in the morning."

"You didn't need to go to the trouble."

"I like baking, and I miss having someone to do it for. I send things along with Cammie, of course, but that only goes so far, and she only comes home one weekend in three or four."

"Where is she in tutoring?"

"A relative of Octavian's - a married aunt up in the Midlands. She's with two cousins, and several others from families they know. They're not hung up on what girls should or shouldn't learn and they've given her a solid foundation. I don't have any complaints about it, except I don't have her around."

"You've a good relationship with her then?" He hoped

so. Some people sent their children to tutoring because they didn't want to be parents.

Pross turned back and nodded. "I like to think so, yes. And we've only got each other. I'd hate to spoil that."

She watched a series of expressions cross his face, before he said, carefully. "I've a younger sister, at Schola. In her fourth year, now. In Owl. Hypatia Ward."

Pross grinned. "The Owlery's grand. I mean, I know I'm expected to say it, but I hope she's happy there."

Ibis tilted his head. "That's the first thing you ask?"

Pross shrugged. "Should it be something else?"

"People usually ask about our parents? Or whether she's half Egyptian."

"I'm sure if you wanted me to know those things, you're quite capable of telling me." She brought the tea over, setting the tray with the pot and cups on the table between them, pulling over the portable desk with her own notes, and then settling into the blue chair. She glanced at him, to discover him watching her, intently.

"You're not what I expected." She looked up, unsure how to take that. Did he have expectations of her? Fortunately, this had an answer she'd given before.

"That would be rather tedious, I'm sure. There are a lot of things people expect reasonably young widows to be. I find most of them - stifling."

That got him blinking at her, as if he was rearranging the heavens in his head, and then a small startled sound, followed by "I'm sure you would."

Pross said cheerfully, "Quite." She reached out to rearrange her things.

"My sister..." Ibis was a little unsure of something, the way his voice sounded. "Our father died a few years ago. He was rather older. Hypatia's the youngest by more than a decade. He was English, Mother is Egyptian. Also older."

Pross watched him. "Hypatia for the philosopher?"

Ibis lit up. "Oh, yes. And thank you for not calling her the last librarian."

"Well, given Alexandria continued as a centre of learning for some goodly time after, I should hope not. But still a fascinating and accomplished woman."

That earned her a small smile. "We've a brother and a sister, back in Egypt with Mother now. Families of their own."

"And you didn't go that road?"

"Not the right time, nor people who'd walk it with me." He flicked his fingers. "That - I told you about Seal, being between places, never fitting in."

"They say that about owls, sometimes. Liminal about time rather than about space."

"I wonder how that fits into the Quadrivium." His voice had turned contemplative now.

Pross laughed. "Well, if you have numbers, numbers in space, numbers in time, numbers in time and space."

He shook his head. "I always rather preferred it as pure, stationary, moving, and applied." he said, thoughtfully. "Anyway. This is not getting our research done."

"No. What did you spot yesterday, then?"

He arched an eyebrow. "Why do you ask?"

"You asked her about water. Wells, cisterns, that sort of thing."

Ibis leaned back, suddenly very relaxed, so she'd said something just right again, to earn that. "I did."

"And you did so for a reason. That wasn't at all in the notes." Now that she'd done a right thing, she had to figure out where to take it.

"Come on, Proserpina." This was decidedly teasing her back now. "You needn't be asking me this."

That got a laugh from her, despite herself, and a "You were setting up a lure for her, weren't you?"

He nodded. "I was. And you'll notice I told no lies. I just asked if she knew anything about a place with water."

"Which anyone who knows anything about - well, where you put houses - would know there has to be somewhere. You said nothing about what was there."

"Well, I expect there's water there. Or was. Water tables being what they are, and the courses of rivers and streams, and the various climate effects."

She raised an eyebrow, and he waved a hand, continuing, "It got a lot colder here, in the late medieaval period. Well, most places. You've heard the stories about ice skating on the Thames, surely?"

Pross nodded and murmured, "And that would affect the water there."

"Water is connected to everything. First law of archaeology, if I had my way."

Pross leaned back, thinking through this. "I saw how she reacted. So keen and grasping, just for a moment."

"I hope she's not a very close friend." His voice turned dry.

Pross shook her head. "A client. Honestly, a rather difficult one, though it's a little hard to know how much of that difficulty is reasonable. Maybe you have a better sense?"

"You, Pross, are my third consulting client since I've been a fellow, and you are quite different from the previous two."

"Is that a compliment?"

"Oh, rather. Six ways round."

That made her laugh and then say, "So what did you spot?"

TEN

TRUE EYEWORTH

I bis took his time, pouring a cup of tea. Pross could tell he was being deliberate about it, drawing out the little fussy movements. "I could ask you to tell me."

"No games, sir." She was prompt about that. "I am not your junior, in this, but your peer."

"Pax, pax." The response was immediate, and he held his hands up. "Beg pardon."

Pross watched him, for a moment, then settled her thoughts and her hands. This duelling of wits, it was something new. Octavian had never been like this, not with her.

Oh, they'd been well-matched. An arranged marriage, designed to harness their better selves into producing new learning and children, and they'd done well with that, with Cammie. They had learned to work well together, the ways her mind and his met, and where one or the other excelled, how to lean this way.

But it had been hard-won at times. Octavian's family had clear ideas about who was head of the household, about how the family worked, that went back to the First Families and the ancient traditions of Rome.

There was nothing wrong with that, but Pross came from a family with a broader experience of the world, an awareness that there were so many wonders, so many magics, so many things to know that British magic, European magic, just brushed over.

She had that sense with Ibis. A far more natural one, intuitive, the way their minds went at the problem in different ways, but leading to the same place. How he could accept that she had her reasons for her way, quite naturally. He had those fits of bafflement or brief defensiveness, but she suspected he had every right. She'd seen the way the hints of his comments suggested others had treated him poorly, or made all the wrong assumptions.

Pross was not sure what to do with this at all. Though, she realised with a start, saying something, anything, was probably a good idea.

She coughed, then murmured, "Granted," before she offered "I would rather work this through together with you."

He nodded, then said "May I ask what you know about, pardon, Philly?"

"Old family in the Forest, they've had that property since thirteen hundred and something. I could look up the date. I did a summary when I took the research on."

"Did she come to you, or was she referred?"

"She came to me. Which isn't that odd. There's a bookstore in Little Beaulieu, that's the magical village, but it doesn't have much research material, and the owner's quite old. More a hobby the past decade or two, not much new stock. And he's always focused on the ships and naval history."

"Which are not relevant to this, no." Ibis nodded.

"Rather not. And I've lived other places, and I've

helped with a couple of other questions. Nothing this complicated before, but I had a sense of how to break it down. And asked for advice, a couple of places."

"Anyone else I'd know?"

Pross considered. "You might know the name, at least. Lord Carillon. That's Geoffrey, who was the youngest son of our generation. He and I were in the Owlery together though he's a few years older. He holds Ytene now. That's where the portal you're taking back to London is."

Ibis blinked. "I've heard the name. Rather dissolute, his reputation."

"Oh, reputation." She snorted. "People say the oddest things. He's settled down. Married a year, a baby on the way. His wife is lovely, most clear headed, I've enjoyed getting to know her the past two years. My best friend is wife to the head of his stables so I'm over there sometimes, or she comes here."

"He plays pavo, doesn't he? He's the sort that would."

"He's honestly a joy to watch on a horse. And he treats his people quite well." That came out sounding a bit defensive. "Also, as I said, he has a portal. They don't open it up to general traffic, but I made arrangements for you to go through."

"Why doesn't he open it up?"

"Security-minded, he is. I haven't actually asked, but I wouldn't be surprised if he'd been in Intelligence at least part of the War. And it's right off their main courtyard. Very handy in an emergency, but you don't want carts coming and going at all hours. Ytene is about the top half of the Forest, in terms of oath-ties."

Ibis thought about that, then said, cautiously, "I hadn't thought much about the layers of maintaining a large estate. Not a problem I've ever had. Father's is small. The manor house, a tiny village, a few houses, a mill, that kind of thing."

"Yours, now, or?"

He grimaced. "Being handled by a steward. I - I don't have a gift for the management. Or for people."

Pross nodded and then determined to change the subject. "I suppose we had better work through the translations in more depth."

"That, yes, and it's easier and..." He hesitated. "More pleasant, in company."

"What is the next step, after that?"

"More research, but I'm now certain we'll want to go out there. Can you make travel arrangements, or should I look into it?"

"Let me do a little investigating and then write? Maybe train's easier than other options."

They settled amiably into the details of the text, pausing for elevenses, and then wrapping up with many more notes and half a dozen books each to review.

"I wonder," he said, as they were wrapping up. "There are some texts in the Bibliotheque in Paris that might shed some light on some of those notes about possible inscriptions. I admit a little worry that we'll find the thing and then discover something that keeps us out."

"You mean the thing that might be some sort of lock, or ward?"

Ibis nodded. "I can see about going to Paris, perhaps." His voice trailed off. Then, almost hesitantly, he continued, "Would you tell me a little about the shop? Do we have a minute?"

She nodded and then considered where to start. "Octavian's parents live not too far from here. Up near Salisbury. Ten miles or so, a reasonable enough distance, even without a portal. We moved here when the shop came open. The woman who had it before, she was ready to retire, and Octavian could consult from anywhere, he did manuscript repair, research, half a dozen things, but mostly by post."

"Wanted somewhere quieter, after the War?" Ibis's voice was quiet.

"That too. London was too much for him, all the people, the noise, the... different things happening. This village, you know what to expect, mostly. Who you'll see, what the rhythm of the day is."

She turned on her heel. "Anyway, the shop is the ground floor, most of it open for browsing, though there's a storage room at the back, some storage in the basement, and we use the third bedroom upstairs for an office and guest room." She took a breath. "If we'd had other children, but..." She shrugged. "A lot of things didn't come out like we expected."

Ibis opened his mouth, then said, carefully, "May I ask what happened to Octavian? Or is that too personal?"

Pross glanced up, and Ibis looked very sincere. Not the sort of prying question a lot of people might ask, where they were trying to tell their own fears to shut up, but honestly curious.

"A bad heart. Freak thing, they said, nothing he could have known about, in advance. Done anything about. I don't know if they were telling us that to be - kind?"

"I was brought up with Mother's house gods," he said, "Roughly. Egypt is different about a lot of things. Father's - structure, sort of, Mother's approach." He swallowed. "Anyway. We believe that anyone whose name is remembered, still lives. Temples. Shrines. Tombs. Letters. Writing. Any of it."

Pross tilted her head, then said, quietly. "I knew that in

my head, but thank you for saying it." And then more briskly. "We were a made-match. Each of us given a handful of people of suitable background who might be a fit, and a matchmaker to help us get to know each other. We didn't start out madly in love or anything, but we... I miss him a lot, still."

"And he wanted you to have the bookshop?"

That startled her, but she nodded. "I... he never said that. But you're right, he did. He wanted... he wanted me to have a place to be. Where I could do things."

"Show me around?" Ibis was very intent, now.

She had to catch her breath, but then she walked him through to the door of the shop, her polished old wood desk. "Here, the entrance, I want things to be engaging. That's where I am most of the day. Sending out orders, doing paperwork, or if that's done, reading. A lot of my work is ordering copies for people, tracking down copies - those are the catalogues - but I also recommend things to people, and that's much easier to do if I've read them."

"Is there a library near here?"

"Salisbury, for a magical one. They send around a cart with books on it every fortnight, but the choice is a bit catch as catch can."

"And over here?"

"This is the non-fiction. Mostly popular works, biographies, overviews, that kind of thing. Not too dense. And here's the fiction, divided by type."

"Do you have a favourite?"

She looked up, watching him watch her, and then she said "Some of the mysteries. Especially the series where you can see characters over time. I like that part a lot. Agatha Christie, if you read non-magical authors. She's brilliant. Only a few books out so far, but interesting."

"You sell both?"

"Mmhmm. More magical than not here, but a bit of both. And there're protections on the magical texts, to make sure they don't get out into the wider world."

"What sort of things do you have there?"

"Well, some practical texts, of course - herbals and household magics and all. But also children's books. Here's one - a book about the flora and fauna of the New Forest. I always keep a copy in stock now, a good luck charm. That's part of how Ferry - my best friend - and her husband Rufus met."

She turned to get the book out to show him, and then suddenly, he was leaning in toward her. It seemed like time stopped, as if he might be about to kiss her, or murmur something provocative in her ear, or touch her cheek.

And then he did none of those, as if he managed to catch himself just before he dove off a cliff. A moment later, he was shifting onto his heels, all the properness snapping back into place. "I'd be glad to buy it from you. Learn more about the Forest, beyond what I've seen."

She let out a long breath and then said, "Don't feel you must. But if you'd like to, I'd be a poor sort of bookseller to turn you down."

Fussing over the coin and the receipt gave them both a little time to find their footing again, and then she could say, "It's a mile walk, the roads should be all right."

"Do lead on." Ibis shrugged into his cloak.

It was a reasonably pleasant walk, for the tail end of January, and she made occasional comments about the area and the people as they went, nothing nearly as personal as their earlier conversation. He helped by asking questions, or encouraging her to tell one local story or another. Once they got to Ytene, there were more things to talk about. Ferry came out to meet them, and Lizzie to open the portal. The lord of the manor was apparently elsewhere, on some project.

Ibis bowed over her hand. "I'll write. If you'd look into the arrangements for getting up to the site. We won't be able to go until the end of March or maybe April, depending on the weather, and be able to do much out of doors, so there's no particular rush."

Pross snorted. "I explained that to Philly, yes. But it will let us follow up the other leads."

"Quite. I'd planned to see my sister in a couple of weeks, and I'll see about checking the Schola library, maybe asking one of my old teachers who might have some ideas. I'll let you know what I find out."

Pross nodded, trying to figure out what to say next. "I'll look forward to your letter, then. Safe travels, good hunting."

She caught a hint of a smile as Ibis turned to go through the portal.

ELEVEN

LATE FEBRUARY, AN ISLAND OFF THE COAST OF WALES

I t was almost the end of February before Ibis arranged
the visit to Schola. He stepped through the portal and
inhaled deeply. It felt wonderful to breathe in the sea air,
feel the breeze, and look up at the bulk of the castle that
held the school itself. It was all quite impressive, in an
exceedingly British way.

Setting foot here always felt so strange, not because it
was bad, but because it felt so natural, like diving into the
water and knowing you could breathe. Or the solidness of
the ground beneath his feet, shaped by generations of
students and teachers. Magic felt more potent here.

He'd come early, to look at the library. His sister had
been quite clear she would be glad to see him, but she had a
variety of other plans for a rare long weekend besides seeing
her older brother. He made his way over to the library
building, set into the surrounding walls of the castle, looking
out over the bay and back toward the mainland.

At the entrance to the reading room, he nodded to the
librarian, a woman perhaps in her late twenties. A different
woman than the older witch he'd known during his own

school days. She had him sign the proper forms and directed him to one of the visitor desks, set well away from the student areas. Once he was settled, she wheeled over the cart of items he'd requested.

He set to work, diligently, making the most of his time with the practised eye to research that he'd learned over the years, triaging the materials. These were things he needed to skim and make sure there was no chapter or section dealing with his topics. These had a relevant chapter but he need only look at that one chapter. And these might have other references.

Unfortunately, none of the sources seemed to have what he needed. Until, that is, he came across one that had not been on his list of requests, a text from the ninth century. It appeared to be a journal about finding metals.

He took it over to the desk, and murmured "Pardon, miss? This wasn't on my list, but it looks very promising. Can you tell me more about the provenance?"

"The Library thought it would be useful."

Ibis blinked, then said, "Yes, ma'am. The provenance? So I can put it in proper context."

The librarian stood up, going to a series of drawers behind the desk. She drew out a neatly written card, placing a blank card behind it, and tapped the paper with a particular flick of her fingers. She brought the copy back, with a, "This is what we know, sir."

He glanced at the card, then nodded. "I appreciate it." And then a "Um. Is it proper for me to express my appreciation to the Library?"

That earned him a warmer smile, and a "If you would make a suitable note in the book, there. The guest book. That would be appreciated. Details particularly, to the degree you can share them."

Ibis nodded, and withdrew, not entirely sure what to do with that, and went back to his desk, with the notes. The card she had given him had a few more details about the original owner, and about how it had come into the collection. He'd have to check Pross's notes about Philly's family, but he thought the journal had come from a distant relative. It certainly had more specifics than they'd found elsewhere.

At ten to four, he wrapped up his notes, and returned to the desk. "Thank you, ma'am, for your help. If I need to come back and look at that volume again, may I request it?"

"With the proper forms, but you have the process down," she said. "May I shelve the rest?"

"Thank you, yes."

There was a pause, then the librarian said, "Ibis Ward. Do you have a relative here?"

"My youngest sister, Hypatia. I'm about to take her for tea in the village."

That got a nod, and, "You've the same look, about the face." She gave him a considering look, and then said "You're welcome to come back and visit, of course. Anyone who cares about research is."

Ibis blinked, then nodded. "Thank you," he said again, a little baffled. "Good afternoon." And then he withdrew, leaving a brief but appropriate note in the guest book. As he came out the door to the courtyard, he spotted his sister coming out of the Owlery, and waved.

She broke away from her friends with a comment he couldn't hear, and then walked briskly over to him, with an insistent dignity. Two years ago, she'd have hugged him, and he missed that. Instead, he got a nod and a "Ibis" and then a rush of Arabic, that made him laugh, and say "You know the rules."

She groaned. "English."

"You never know who can overhear and understand," he said, solemnly. "Come on, let's go get a splendid tea."

They walked down out of the courtyard, around the curve to the village, a pleasant three-quarters of a mile. Enough that the sense of the school receded a little. He felt a little rush of nostalgia, but his hunger drew them on.

Once they settled in a nook in the tea room, Ibis checked the privacy magics. "Now we may speak freely."

That got a laugh. "You know it was just the gossip."

"You can never tell when some bit of gossip gets dangerous." He tried to look serious. It didn't work.

"You try to scold, brother, and you know you can't ever stick to it."

"Hypatia....." His voice trailed off.

"You know I'm right. So how did the research go?"

"It wasn't as helpful as I'd hoped. Except for one book that - the librarian said the Library gave it to me?"

"Young librarian or old librarian?"

"Not Mistress Anders. Dark hair, maybe late twenties?"

"That's Mistress Loft. And she's thirty-two and not yet married."

He blinked. "Pardon. How is that relevant?"

"She asked me about you, after you made the request to visit. What you were doing. How old you were. You know. The things people ask if they're maybe interested."

"I don't know." Ibis felt lost. Not that that was an uncommon feeling with Hypatia. "You know I'm not good with that."

"What did she say to you, all of it?"

Ibis repeated their few exchanges. He thought he'd recalled them. When he got to the part about being invited back, Hypatia went "Hah!"

"Explain?"

"That means she'd like an excuse to see you again. She's making it easy."

He blinked. "You. That can't be right."

"Tell me about your Mrs Gates. How things are going." It was an abrupt shift, but of course Hypatia wasn't as deft at that sort of thing as Ibis was. Or their mother, for that matter.

That made him pause, and suddenly he realized that he didn't want to explore the topic. Even with his sister. She might be younger, but she had a sense of observation about people he never had had. Despite that, he didn't want to set out Mrs Gates and her every action for her dissection. It was why he didn't like gossiping.

"She's very thorough." It came out softly.

"Come on, brother. That's not much, and you know it."

He paused, then tried something else. "I like how she thinks through problems."

"Tell me about your trip out there, in person. Your letter didn't say much."

Ibis paused, and talked about it, step by step. Arriving at the inn, the odd ride in the back of Philly's cart. Hesitantly, he talked about how the armaments room felt very foreign, suddenly, all the assumptions built into it. His father's estate had a room sort of like that, for the papers, but it didn't feel that way. Some things in England felt comfortable to him, and others made him feel like he was on the surface of some far distant planet, unable to understand anything. He could gesture at it, poorly, but Hypatia was much more a child of England than he was, and it didn't make sense to her.

It was easier to describe what they found in the papers, than how Pross looked when she was researching, the way she'd leaned into her work. He found himself talking about how she leaned forward, the little trick she had to keep her hand out of the line of notes while the ink dried, the small charm she used to help.

He got around to the next day, their conversation, and said "I wrote that, I think, that she hopes you're enjoying the Owlery."

"Not what you expected her to say?"

"No. I didn't know how to explain."

"That it's been hard for all of us? We're not the type of colonial connections people expect."

"No. But I think maybe she'd understand."

"What happened next?"

That made him blush. "She showed me a book - a good luck charm, she said, to have a copy, it had helped one of her friends meet her husband. I mean, the friend's husband." He stumbled over the words.

His sister leaned forward, leaning her chin on her hand. "And?"

"I bought a copy. And I..." There was a moment of slow dawning horror and amazement. "Was she? Did she think I was?"

What he heard next was his sister laughing, a sound of pure delight. Fortunately, they were interrupted by the arrival of a proper cream tea with all the fussy dishes and cake and sandwich trays. By the time the staff were finished, Hypatia had at least stopped breaking into giggles every other breath.

He poured, took a sandwich, and then looked up, abashed.

"You could ask her, brother."

"She's a widow. She still wears her ring. Some people have decency."

Hypatia was about to say something, and Ibis interrupted her, in a sudden rush. "That's not kind, to make her uncomfortable. I know people do it to you, and I'm sure they've done it to her, a few things she's not really said. But that isn't a reason I should do it, that's not kind, and she deserves kindness and decency and not me gossiping over her like, like..."

"Like a schoolgirl." Hypatia was apologetic. "I'm sorry. You're right."

Ibis watched her for a long minute, then said, "I like working with her. I don't want to... damage that. And she's a good scholar. She puts her skills down, that she's just a bookseller, her husband was the researcher, but she is solidly good."

Hypatia nodded, then took a breath and brought up a puzzle in her current coursework on ritual. He listened for a few moments, asking the sort of easy questions any relative might. Then she admitted the problem.

"It's that protective ritual work. You remember, Ummi said I could." She was adapting a traditional practice of their mother's for protection of a home to the British climate. That led to a long enough discussion of divine powers outside their native lands that it was nearly six when Ibis realised the time.

"I need to walk you back, I'm meeting Master Hase at half-six."

"The master of your old house?"

Ibis nodded. "I have something to ask him about. Not you, obviously."

"Well, I've no coursework with him, I should hope not. I should get back, though, I have astronomy work to do once it's dark and I still need to set up the noteboard for it."

"How are you set for the Festival of Renewal? I meant to ask earlier."

"Oh, brother, honestly." Hypatia was all amused frustration. "You think I won't remember."

"Well, it takes a little preparation. And you know Mother fusses."

"I've a workroom reserved, and you sent the incense last month, and I've the other things. You've asked, I've told you, let it be." Hypatia was sharp now.

Ibis nodded, paid for their tea, and they walked back up the road, toward the castle lights. When he left her at the gate, to turn down the path to the cottage along the coast, Hypatia said "I am sorry for teasing."

The kiss she left on his cheek before she turned and walked off startled him almost as much as the apology.

TWELVE

SCHOLA

I bis presented himself at the cottage at exactly half-six, as Master Hase had said. He'd never actually been here before, at Master Hase's personal cottage, just the rooms that went along with the house master position. He knew, intellectually, that most of the staff at Schola had their own cottages on the island, passed down within their fields or families or connections of affection and mentorship. Seeing one was something different, though.

The cottage was along the road to the playing fields, rather than nearer the shore, which he thought rather a curious thing, given Hase was master of Seal House.

"Come."

Hase's voice sounded much the same as he remembered it. When Ibis entered, he blinked a little, at the light. Hase was sitting by the fire, in a comfortable chair, another one set at an easy conversational distance. He was naturally older than when Ibis was in school, but he looked older than Ibis had expected, going silver by his ears and throughout the short beard, and quite tired.

"Sir?"

"Do come in, Ward. I had them bring tea down, and sandwiches. I wasn't sure if you'd have eaten?"

"Very kind, sir." Ibis came in further, closing the door behind him. "And thank you for making the time."

"You've asked for rather less of it than most of your peers, and I'm glad to offer. And as you see, I am not on duty tonight."

"Sir." And then Ibis had to ask "I was never entirely sure how that worked, sir."

"Ah, that's a mystery we might probe at a later date, if you're curious. You had a particular question for me, didn't you?"

Ibis nodded. "I did." He settled in the chair meant for him, and reached for his portfolio, stopping when Hase shook his head. "We have time for specifics later. Tell me the centre of it."

It felt like being back in an examination again, one of those where it was not just knowledge that would see you through, but how you presented your choices. Ibis closed his eyes, against yet another in an endless series of tests. He had to trust that Master Hase had some reason for doing this, and this way.

"A researcher brought a question to me, that concerns a possible Roman hoard in Norfolk. The records available suggest that it may have one or more magical items, but there are oddities in the case."

"A researcher you've worked with before?"

"No, sir. She's an Owl, a widow, a bookseller by trade. Her husband was a fellow of the Research Society before the War."

"Not your period, surely? Nor country."

"No, sir." Ibis felt like he couldn't explain any of this well.

"Are you enjoying helping her?"

The answer was on his lips and out of his mouth before he had time to think. "Yes, sir. I like her questions, her focus, her approach. And it's a good chance to learn more about the possible archaeological puzzles here."

"Since you're likely to be here at least a few more years, yes?"

"Sir, yes, until my sister finishes her apprenticeship, if all goes well."

Hase nodded, before he murmured, "Go on."

"I wanted your advice, sir, on two pieces. You mentioned, when I was in school, a familiarity with the area of Norfolk, near Aylsham."

"I was tutored near there, yes. And I go back some summers. Cousins," Hase said. "You have an excellent memory, Ward."

"I do pay attention, sir. I'm told it's one of my better virtues."

That earned him a warmer laugh, and Ibis relaxed slightly.

"What did you want my help with?"

"I know you've taken an interest in Norfolk history, sir, so any suggestions. And then there was another question. I'm not sure who else to ask, sir."

"About the hoard, or something else?"

"Someone at the Research Society, sir."

That earned him a raised eyebrow. "You do bring me interesting questions, Ward." He waved a hand. "I am glad to entertain both. As I said, you have rather a reserve of help available to you."

They settled into a proper discussion of the hoard, the various points Ibis and Pross had sorted out so far. Master Hase eventually permitted Ibis to bring out his sketches. Ibis set them out, to explain the various logical derivations of some of their research based on elevation maps and descriptions of the landscape in different eras.

Hase made a suggestion. Ibis smiled. "Sir, that would have made sense, except this river changed course in a flooding season in 1103. If the villa were there, they'd have seen signs of it when the bank washed out."

That earned him a laugh, and a "I should not teach you to suck eggs, then. Right. What about this one?"

They took an hour to work through the different options, in the end, they had narrowed down the likeliest location for the villa to three spots to investigate further. Hase knew the country quite well, it turned out, having rambled over most of it at various points, and he knew the signs of ruins underground. They talked through what to look for, the blackberry and bramble patches that might indicate stone near the surface, or the mysterious hollows that didn't quite fit the landscape. They were all quite close to each other, within half a mile from Philly's old family estate.

"There. I think I have been as much help here as I can be. What about your other question?"

Ibis had to catch his breath. "It's more complicated, sir."

"We are Seal, we are good with complications." Hase said it easily but Ibis could feel the solidity behind that, the way Hase would not let him duck asking.

"Someone I work with at the Research Society. I caught something... unexpected, in a conversation. A flash of something. Not an overlay, quite, but distinct."

"Do you have a description of what it was like?"

"Scales on a snake, sir, was the thing I thought of. Or the bubbles from a hippopotamus or crocodile, just under the water, in the river."

"Something dangerous, then?"

Ibis nodded. "Something dangerous."

"That's most interesting, Ward. Have you had that sense about people before? Did you, at school?"

Ah, here was the tricky part to answer. "Sometimes, sir. But I don't know..." He paused. "My mother's family, the way they do magic, it's not as they teach it here. Some of it is formal ritual, architecture, alignment. But some of it is a more instinctive, or at least more tied to natural cycles."

"And you are not sure where this thing comes to you from. When did you notice it?"

"A few times at school, sir. A few times with you, sir, not always? But that is..." Ibis stopped. "You are the only person I could think of to ask, sir."

"Ah, Ibis. You could have asked years ago." Master Iase's voice was gentle. "With others?"

"More in our house, sir, than other people, but not everyone in our house? Or all the time." He paused, and added, "That would have been exceedingly distracting, sir."

"And did you notice it in this man before?"

"No, sir. But I try not to spend much time in his company, sir."

"Does he not care for you, or do you not care for him?"

Again, Ibis was not sure how to answer, how to explain this. "Both, sir," he said after a long pause. "I find him trivial, sir. He likes lunches with wealthy people, and wandering in late, and being invited to cocktail parties."

"And that offends you as a researcher, doesn't it?"

"Sir." Ibis flushed, and looked down and away, into the fire.

"Oh, quite understandable. How does the man make you feel?"

This was too much, too pressing. Ibis looked sharply over at his former house master, and Hase immediately held up his hands. "I do not mean to... we are horrible at talking about emotions, aren't we? I meant other senses, more than emotion. Does it feel like something in particular? Water or air or warmth or cold or something else?"

"Slippery, sir." Ibis had the word in his mind immediately. "But not with slime or damp, but something dry. Scales, almost. Harder. Sharper."

Hase nodded. "I'd be interested in your future observations. I cannot judge precisely what the cause is, not without meeting the man. Perhaps we might arrange something, over the spring holidays? If there is a lecture or something in London he might attend? In the meantime, whatever you see and feel, make a note, and we can evaluate it together. You are welcome to make a further appointment at any time."

Ibis nodded. "I should not take more of your time, sir." He half stood.

"Oh, that was not me telling you to go. That was me telling you when to come back. Stay. Tell me about your other research at the moment. Or I have a question, a matter of my alchemical work, a student had a project that made me think of you."

"Sir?"

"Are you so unsure of your welcome?"

Ibis swallowed, then nodded. "Generally, sir, it is safest to assume that at best I am tolerated and must earn my place."

Hase looked at him for a long moment. "I cannot claim

to understand, but I will tell you as plainly as I can, you are one of mine, and you are welcome."

Ibis did not understand what to do with that, and yet, he could not be rude. He murmured, "Thank you for saying so, clearly, sir." before he could retreat into the nuanced magical discussion of alchemical formulae.

THIRTEEN

TRUE EYEWORTH

"It's been months." Cammie was curled up in the purple chair, hands cupped around a mug of steaming hot cocoa, dark curls coming out every which way.

"Two months, you. Since you were here, anyway." Pross finished rinsing out the pot and sat down.

"We were in London, in January."

"And at your great-aunt's for the long weekend in February."

"And now it's the middle of March. Why do I have a holiday?"

"Because it's the equinox, and they have family things. Same as last year."

"I'll be so bored. Two whole weeks." Cammie drew the last two words out.

"You have rooms of books downstairs. And assignments to work on. Don't think Madam Martin didn't tell me you needed to brush up on several things if you're going to have a pleasant time next year."

Cammie stuck out her tongue, which Pross found very reassuring. She had worried that her daughter had got too solemn, too grown up, too young. If nothing else the tutoring seemed to have been a great help there, giving her more balance.

"But there's no one around. Everyone else is off at school. Caelus and Cardea and Delphie."

"More time for reading. And your assignments."

"Mother." Cammie drew out the word again.

"If you're that bored, you can help me do the inventory."

"No, no, I'll find something to do." Cammie was quick to back off.

Pross laughed and leaned back. "And we can go spend a day or two with Ferry. So. You said you had a question when I got you from the portal."

"About your research. You promised you'd tell me about it, and then you didn't. I asked twice."

"I tried, but it didn't go into letters tidily."

Cammie swung a leg over the arm of the chair. "And you hate untidy letters."

"You know I do."

"What is untidy about it?"

Pross leaned back. "It's a curious puzzle. We're trying to track down, I told you this part, a possible Roman hoard in Norfolk. We know roughly where it should be, but it's a large estate, and it could be in a couple of different locations on the land."

"You mentioned that the landscape had changed."

"That's why I needed an archaeologist. Or someone who could decipher some of the Latin. Or someone, maybe, who could go at it from the materia side, finding what's buried."

"By looking for buried things, buried magical things. You explained that part."

"I wasn't sure what stuck. You had rather been going on about the unfairness of examinations."

Cammie straightened and said with a remarkable amount of injured dignity, "There are expectations for a student in my position, mother."

Pross laughed. "Anyway, he came here, to see the document in situ, as it were."

"What did he make of Philly?" Pross arched an eyebrow, and Cammie grimaced and said, "Mrs Tipson."

"I want you to be polite, ta. I think she rather baffled him. You remember how she is, all what-ho and noisy good cheer."

"And the chickens."

"The chickens are a constant, yes."

Cammie nodded. "And you said he stayed over?"

"We took the evening cart run up here, and he stayed in the inn." Pross paused. "Got a talking to from George - Mr Walker - after, for not warning him."

"Warning him?"

"That Mr Ward is half-Egyptian."

"Why would that need a warning?"

"Some people can't keep a civil tongue in their head without help, apparently." That came out sharper than she meant.

Cammie frowned, chewing on that.

"Because he looks different?"

"It's not just looks. He grew up in a different community, a different culture. I looked him up, his family came back here before he went to Schola, when he was about your age."

That earned her a thoughtful silence. "Do you think Mr Walker was nasty, or someone else?"

"We're still a small village. The men who went off to

fight, they met people from all over, but many people who've been here for ages don't know much else. Sometimes that's scary."

"Is that why they're rude?"

"Maybe. It's not like I asked everyone. Or anyone, really. I'm not sure they'd tell me if I did." She paused and diverted from the question of being an outsider into explaining the more important part for her daughter. "Being scared isn't an excuse, but it helps to understand why people do a thing if you want them to change it. Or if you have to deal with them."

"Is that why you're working with Mr Ward and not someone else?"

"Well, I suspect they pushed me off on him because he couldn't refuse, he didn't have the status to. And I'm a nobody from a tiny village who won't throw a fit, yes."

"Only it turns out you get on."

"So far, yes. And we see to be a good fit for the research, which is the actually relevant part."

Cammie settled in with her cocoa, taking a few sips before she said, "So do you have to work while I'm home?"

"There is a bookshop, yes." Pross let her voice turn dry.

"That's not work, Mum."

"Three new boxes of inventory is in fact work, thank you." Pross couldn't be that upset.

"Three boxes means you sold things. That's good!"

"Very, for my paying your tutoring. I'll be glad next year, when it's just your books and supplies."

Cammie was sober for a few moments before she asked. "What else, with the store?"

"I had someone asking to apprentice, but there's not enough work for two. Well, not unless the research part picks up a lot."

"And?" Cammie was leaning forward, curious.

"And I'm not sure I want it to. This, what I'm doing, that's a good amount. I can still read books and tend the shelves and help books find their people and people find their books. That's the part I've always liked."

"Papa was..." Cammie's voice turned cautious, as it often did when her father's name slipped out before her thoughts caught up.

Pross just waited. It was no good rushing this part.

"Papa liked the research so much."

"He did. He wanted to do that with all his time, and then some."

"And you don't like it that much?"

Pross rearranged herself in her chair, considering. "That's part of... I think that's part of why going away to school is good. So you can see different ways of doing things. Parents are two ways, and the other people you see growing up."

"That's not an answer."

Pross could hear the edge in Cammie's voice, the edge that could turn bad for both of them.

"Give me a moment, all right?"

It earned her a sulky nod, and Pross took a minute to gather her words. "You know I love your father. Did and do. But we were... we worked together one particular way. Very logical, step by step. And that worked for the two of us together."

Cammie nodded slowly, then said, "But? I can hear a but."

"But," Pross agreed. "He isn't here anymore. And I could do that with him, but I can't do it as well without him." She gestured at the stairs, down to the bookshop. "Do you know why we're doing better?"

"No?" Cammie shook her head. "You don't tell me details, Mum."

"I should make you go down and look at the shelves." Pross said, cheerfully. "Make it into a proper puzzle for you. But you only just got home, and it would be a shame to let the cocoa get cold."

Cammie grinned at that. "Good."

Pross gestured downstairs again. "If I made you do that, you'd see that..." She paused, for words. "Your father's idea of a bookshop was orderly. And he wasn't wrong - if you can't find a book, you can't sell it."

"That makes sense."

"It does. Only, lists and books in alphabetical rows don't tell you all the things about a shop. It was something Madam Howell said."

"The Mistress you apprenticed with." Cammie wanted to make sure of the name.

"Yes. I know you don't remember her well, she died when you were so young. But I woke up one night, and I'd had such a dream of her. A week or two after you went off, last autumn."

Cammie tilted her head. "You said nothing about it?"

"You were busy with all your friends. And it was the kind of dream I wanted to think about a lot."

"What was it about?"

"It was a long conversation about a store being, well, a conversation between all the things in it. Or a library, she'd got the idea from a librarian she knew. How you wanted to have things that showed you different aspects, had different parts of the picture."

Cammie chewed on her fingernail for a moment, and Pross didn't tell her to stop, because the conversation was more important.

"What did you do?"

Pross laughed. "Because clearly I did something?"

"First, you had a dream. Second, something changed, because you said the shop is doing better. Ergo, you have implied that the dream caused a change in your actions." Cammie blinked and looked disgusted. "Now I sound like my logic text."

"You do, rather, but I'm glad it's somewhere in your head."

That earned her the tongue again.

"That very day, I pulled lots of things off the shelves, and rearranged them, and made them into different groups. More like conversations between the books. I made lots of lists but I sent out the lists in different ways, different themes. Not the same old boring ones, like history, or practical spells for the household, but a mix of things. And it turns out that people liked that."

"You sent me those. I liked the rooms of the house set. Kitchen and bathroom and all that."

"Many people did. That's the kind of thing. Thinking about cooking, and about kitchen herbs, and about where our food comes from, or the history of different meals, or how to raise pigs."

Cammie thought about that. "So not so much like Papa did?"

"The lists I use to keep track of things are like he did, and the bookkeeping. But I'm trying different things with the way they are in the shop. It seems to work."

Cammie nodded, and then seemed inclined to chew on it in silence. After a few minutes Pross went about the various tasks of tidying up and washing the mugs and preparing things to cook for supper.

FOURTEEN

TRUE EYEWORTH

It had taken hours and hours for Ibis to get himself anywhere useful.

He'd thought it was a good idea, going to Norwich, to get a sense of the landscape and the site. It was still early in the year to consider any active excavation work. The roads were muddy and the fields were worse.

Getting there had gone smoothly enough, a portal to the nearest magical village, just south of Norwich itself, then a brief walk, two miles, to the Tipson property. He'd done his research well in advance, there was a public bridle path, and a right of way across part of the land. He'd stayed entirely on the public paths.

Only then everything had gone wrong.

He'd taken off, his dignity entirely forgotten, to run back to Norwich, avoiding the portal and taking the train instead. He spent the entire trip hoping that his difficulties wouldn't think to look for him there, in the non-magical side of the world.

And then, from London, a portal from Southwark to Salisbury. A long wait, then one of the informal buses down into the New Forest, and a walk from the non-magical village he'd been dropped in.

By the time he reached True Eyeworth, it was past dark, he was well and truly soaked. His shoulder was aching from his bag, and he was sure his feet were all over blisters, besides worrying his glasses had got cracked.

All he could think of, though, was getting to Pross before she heard about it other ways, or they could get to her. He wasn't sure which would be worse.

He knocked on the door of the bookshop. It was locked, and there were no lights on downstairs. He took a step back, trying to decide what to do. There were lights on upstairs, surely that meant Pross was still awake.

It took forever for the door to open, and when it did, it was not Pross. It was a girl younger than Hypatia. She was definitely surprised, dark curls shaking, and the glare in her eyes standing out against brown skin.

She took a breath, then said, "We're closed." Clear and firm.

"Please, is Pross - Mrs Gates - in?"

The girl looked back at him and didn't budge. "We're closed."

"Please." It came out more plaintive than he wanted.

"You are?"

"Ibis Ward. She knows me. We're working on a project together." He swallowed, trying to get his sense of composure back in the same county he was in, at least. "You - you must be Cammie?" She looked like her mother in the shape of her face, and the blue eyes.

The girl relented. "You. Stand there. If you press up against the side, the rain won't get you. Well, not as much." She then considered and pressed an umbrella through the door before she closed it with a "Back in a couple."

He could hear something turn, a lock, but she had at least given him a little shelter from the rain.

A minute passed, then two, and then the door was opening, and Pross stuck her head out. "Oh, goodness, it is you. Come in. You..." She caught a good look at him then, in the light, and she said, "You look awful. And did someone hit you? There's, is that a bruise on your cheek?"

Ibis shrugged. "No one's been here?"

"Just Cammie. Who is making cocoa by way of apology. And she'll be making one in words too."

Ibis was baffled for a moment, at the sternness in Pross's voice. "Apology?"

"For making you stand out in the rain. Here, let me take your coat. And your bag. Coat here, to dry off, in the vestibule. And yes, an apology, I have done my best to bring her up better than that."

"Strange man, foreign man, turning up in the dark." Ibis ventured a reason Cammie might have been cautious.

"I've told her about you. And besides, it's, we're supposed to be generous to those who wander."

"Xenia?" It was odd what his brain latched onto. It sounded, for a moment, like some of what Master Hase had said, about having resources he hadn't drawn on.

"My name's Roman, but my mum's side of the family is Greek, originally. Welcome the traveller. You never know who it might be. Here, now let's get you upstairs."

Ibis let her guide him up the stairs, into the purple chair. Cammie was indeed making cocoa, and brought it over, just as he sat down. "I'm very sorry. Mum's made it clear leaving you out in the rain was horrid. I'll be going to make up the guest room, now."

She was gone before he could untangle the implications

of that. He'd have thought her a ghost except that, in his experience, ghosts rarely left hot chocolate for you.

Finally, he said, baffled. "Room?"

"You can't go out in that again tonight - even if you wanted to, I'm sure the road will flood by the bridge. I won't make you deal with the inn again, and our couch needs a spring fixed. We have a guest room, there's no reason you shouldn't use it."

He blinked several times. "I'm intruding."

"You turned up here, rather frantic from what Cammie said. We're colleagues, I have a guest room, and Cammie's here to chaperone. If it's a problem, I can see if there's room at the inn, but..." Her voice turned dubious.

Ibis could not face the inn, the staring. No. And she was offering him something, something he hadn't thought possible.

He swallowed, then covered it with a sip of the cocoa, before he said, "If you're sure. I have a change of clothes in my bag, but - not much to sleep in."

"I'll hunt something out. And we can set your things out to dry." She shifted in the chair. "What are you so afraid of?" Her voice turned steady, firm, unrelenting.

He had to steel himself to talk about it. "I went up to Caistor St Edmund, Philly's family property. I should have asked first, but it was all public paths. I thought no one would mind, and it was a nice day up there, I like to get out of London once a week and walk somewhere." He could feel the words rushing through him, tumbling out.

Pross glanced down at his feet, which were at least in sensible walking shoes, then blinked. "Oh, those are... we should let your feet rest."

She stood before he could stop her, and then there was several minutes of bustling around for a footbath. She had some sort of powder to go in it that smelled of mint and felt wonderful when he put his feet in to soak. These kinds of comforts were lacking in a bachelor flat, even one which also contained a medical student.

When she settled down again, after refilling his cocoa and bringing over some sandwiches clearly left from their supper, she said, "There. Tell me, now."

"I was on the public paths, I'd been circling the property as neatly as I could. I made a few sketches, you know, trying to get a sense for where the hoard might be, the lines of the hills."

"That technique of Arbuesson's you sent the article about?" Her voice was even and calming.

Ibis nodded. "And I tried that charm of Kinley's, the one about sensing the age of things? I'd brought the stones for it, and the yew wood and copper."

"I still think that copper's the wrong metal, and you want iron."

The academic wrangling settled him more than the cocoa. "Sometime, we can do a proper test. Though - possibly not in Norwich. I am rather afraid I may have spoiled everything." He was at least calming down. He couldn't tell if it was how Pross was handling him, or the footbath, or the sandwich, or the cocoa, or all of it.

"What happened?"

"I was on the path, trying the different techniques, and I heard a shotgun blast go off. It made me jump, and then I saw two people coming down from the tree line."

Pross had flinched at the comment about the gun, he could see that.

"One was the caretaker, he said. The other, I didn't entirely recognise, it's not as if we exchanged cards, but I could swear he knew me by sight. And not favourably. The caretaker did all the talking. Norwich accent, rough hands, knew his way around the shotgun and then some, had a rather large and toothy dog join him." He shivered.

"Not a dog fan?" It was careful.

"Not the kind who thinks anything on the ground is a toy." Which was true enough. "Or the kind who growls and shows his teeth quite that much."

Pross nodded. "What did they do?"

"Told me to go. I said I was on the public path. They -" He paused. There was no need to tell her the ugliness they'd showered on him. "They were the sort to have the opinion that no one of my apparent background should be on a public path on their land."

Pross made a face like she'd eaten something very bitter. "So you're not telling me what they said."

"The details would not improve your knowledge of the situation." It came out more stilted and dry than he wanted, given all her help so far.

She nodded, quiet for a long moment, before moving on. "Did they hit you? Was anyone else around if we wanted to make a complaint?"

"Yes, and no."

"Salve for your cheek, then? Are you all right? Do you need a Healer? And do you think they'll come here?"

"Nothing that hasn't happened before, no lasting damage." He said it as breezily as he could manage.

"For your last question, something felt very wrong about the whole thing. I'm..." He stopped. "I like to be a rational, logical, thinking man. Not about what I feel that has no evidence. But something felt very wrong. Like being about to step on a snake, you know danger is right there."

"In that case, let me go have a word with our local Guard, he'll be down the pub this time of night." There was a firmness in her tone, that it would take a lot to turn her away from this.

"You've someone here?"

"We had a rather nastier than usual nest of smugglers rounded up a few years ago, and they settled a Guard here after. He's a good sort."

"You're sure it's not a problem for me to stay?"

"No. It's fine. We can feed you in the morning, get you up to the portal."

Ibis was exhausted, and even if he should argue, he couldn't bring himself to. "As you wish, then. Washing up, and telling the Guard, and a bed."

FIFTEEN

TRUE EYEWORTH

Pross was up early, around half-six, well before either Ibis or Cammie were stirring. It gave her time to think.

She'd seen Ibis into the guest room, found him a robe, and told Cammie to stay out his way while he washed up. Then she had put on her rain gear and trudged down the hill to the pub. Joseph Finlan, the Guardsman posted to the village, had at least listened to her and promised that he'd keep an eye out. By the time she came back, the rain was pounding down, and no one who had any sense at all would be out in it. She had locked up again and taken herself to bed with a book.

Now, she busied herself with the small quiet morning things that wouldn't wake anyone. It wasn't until after eight that she heard footsteps, which turned out to be Ibis, in his change of clothes but as proper as he could manage. He'd clearly had a razor and comb in his bag, because he'd cleaned up rather well.

"Morning." Pross made sure her voice was cheerful and warm. The poor man had had a rough day, and an uncertain night. "What sort of things do you like for breakfast? I can do eggs, bacon, potatoes, fried mushrooms, and we've bread and butter and I could put some cheese on it. Whatever combination."

Ibis rubbed his face, clearly still catching up with his circumstances.

"I don't want to be a bother."

"You're not. We like all those things, that's why they're in the kitchen. Tea?"

That earned her more blinking, and then he nodded, asking, "Eggs and bacon, please? And whatever else you'd like to make." She spent the next hour producing food, encouraging him to eat, and welcoming Cammie, who was lured from her bed by the smell of the bacon.

Then it was a matter of writing to Carillon, asking for the loan of the portal and figuring out how to get over there without losing shoes to the mud. That was an interesting challenge, but didn't leave much time for talking, until they were in the paved courtyard.

"I'm worried they'll cause you trouble." The words almost tumbled out of Ibis, in a rush.

"We have wards. And Finlan, the Guardsman, said he'd come by and check things out, and I mentioned to Carillon that someone might be difficult. We're remote here, but not unskilled." She said it as gently as she could. She was finding his worry more charming than annoying, which was rather counter to how she generally felt about people telling her what she ought to be doing.

Ibis looked at her, quiet for a good half minute, before he nodded. "I'll write. You write, too?"

"I still owe you the commentary on that locational magic book you recommend," she said. "I keep bogging down in chapter three. Maybe I'll write it out, and that will help."

That earned her a weak smile, and then the portal was ready, and he had to go through it.

By the time she was back at the bookshop, her legs were soaked up above her knees. At least she'd worn rain boots and could rinse them out and leave them to dry by the fire.

Cammie put the kettle on as soon as Pross got upstairs. She was patient about waiting until her mother had a quick bath and a wash, and had come out in a warm comfortable dress and dry socks and slippers.

"So that's Mr Ward. Did he get off safely?"

Pross said, "We did not come to difficulty in a bog, no. Got off through the portal just fine."

Cammie paused, the little tilt of her head that was like her father, when she was thinking about something, and Pross settled down and waited.

"Is he just a colleague, Mum?" She'd been thinking about the words, the way they came out very precisely.

Pross almost answered immediately, then reconsidered.

"Why do you ask?"

"Because he turned up here. Because you... pay attention to him." Cammie sat down in her chair with a thump. "You thought about making him comfortable."

"He was here after the trip to see Philly. He didn't stay over, but he was up here, talking."

"You didn't ask me before you asked him to stay." That came out in a rush, and Pross closed her eyes for a moment. The kettle went off, which gave them both a chance to gather themselves.

Once they were settled with tea, Pross inhaled it, and then said, "I like him. As a person. He's clever, and thoughtful, and I think people don't pay enough attention to him."

"Attention how?"

Pross tried to figure out how to explain this. "His office, in the Research Society, is up in this little back corner. The kind of place that would have been a junior maid's room when it was a London townhouse. Under the eaves, you can't stand up straight in half of it. And he shares a flat with a medical student."

"Is it that you feel sorry for him?"

Pross had to think about that. "Not pity, no. But..." She paused, then said, "I feel on the outside of things often enough to know what it feels like. And you remember what I told you, about our family, about making visitors welcome."

"Grandmother says that's old superstition."

"Well, I don't do it because I think it's a pair of gods going to show up in a storm. I am fairly certain," she adds after a moment. "And you and I, we're not Baucis and Philemon, now, are we?"

That made Cammie snort, which eased things.

"But that doesn't mean it's not good to be kind. Or to leave space for it." Pross paused, then said, "You remember Judith, my housemate?"

"She's the one who's up in Scotland now, right?"

"Mmhmm." Pross said. "She explained some of her people's customs. There's one specific holy day, where they have a ritual meal. They set a place for someone, a prophet named Elijah, because they have traditions about... well, he might show up. And if he did, you'd want to be ready."

Cammie considered that, long enough to let Pross have several sips of the tea.

"So you're saying that it, that it's a house rule. Being hospitable."

Pross nodded. "It is. A value, anyway. And I'd rather be

the kind of place that welcomes people in, rather than turns them away."

"But what if something bad happens?"

"Where's this coming from, love?"

It came out then, over the course of the next hour of gentle coaxing, about one of her tutoring mates, Amanda. Amanda's father had died a few years ago, complications from War injuries, and her mother had remarried. Bit by bit, Pross got out of Cammie how the stepfather was difficult, and worse than that, had friends who scared Amanda. It wasn't anything they'd done directly, but the way they looked at her, and talked about her when they thought she couldn't hear.

"First," she said, once Cammie had run down. "If Amanda wants to come here, next vacation, that's fine. Or any vacation, with a bit of warning, unless you have to be at your grandparents. Second, if it'd help her to talk to me, about what to do, I can do that."

"Can't you do anything?"

Pross shook her head. "Not without someone asking me. If you want me to come and take both you off for an evening, somewhere we can talk privately, I can do that." It was a long annoying slog to Cammie's tutoring house, from their home. But Pross could and would make that work.

"And if she's really scared, there are people she can talk to. I'll write up a list, all right? Including Mistress Gordon and her husband, but..."

"They know her stepfather. And his friends. So she doesn't dare."

Pross frowned. "And no one's done anything with you?"

Cammie shook her head. "They haven't... I don't think they've done more than scared her? But I don't know if she'd tell me if someone had. It's just..."

Amanda was blonde, of a type most fashionable at the moment, and looked older than she was.

"Let me write and see if Lizzie's free for tea. We can go up there, you can have a ride if the weather clears up, and she might have some ideas, would that help?"

Cammie lit up at that, predictably. A chance to ride the horses at Ytene was a great treat, and an infrequent one outside of summer. She circled back, though, to "Do you like him?"

"Mr Ward? He's very interesting. I like working with him. I don't know what else I think, we've not had that long to talk about anything personal." Pross paused and, considering the conversation they'd just had, asked, "Does he make you feel uncomfortable?"

Cammie thought about it, for several moments, then shook her head. "No, Mum. I was scared, getting the door. He looked so strange and scary when he was all wet. But he was very polite, and I think he was being careful not to scare me more?"

Pross nodded. "He has superb manners. For several reasons, I rather expect. But I'm glad he didn't, once you got over the shock of him turning up like that. Now, love, what do you want me to make for supper, and do you want to help?"

SIXTEEN

LONDON

"W ard."

Ibis did not want to be here. But when the Chief Scholar of the Research Society summoned you, you turned up at the time requested without complaint, wearing the proper clothing. Especially if you were a fellow dependent on his goodwill or at least his benign neglect.

At least Ibis had warning, two hours before the summons, so he could go home and change into the expected sedate suit and pristine shirt and cravat, with the long cape over it. His sole concession to his own culture was the colour of the cravat, a gift from Hypatia, who said it was the same blue as faience, and brought out his eyes.

"Chief Scholar." Ibis nodded and made the hint of a bow that people in Lord Sisley's class found reassuring from people like Ibis. And the title that deferred to his role here, not his birth, as was the custom. Sisley sat in his throne of his chair, his precisely trimmed beard and grey hair entirely in place, formally dressed.

"Sit." It was an instruction, not a request. Ibis could see how this was going. Some men might fight, might demand respect. When he'd been younger, he'd done that, and it had ended badly. He sat.

This room was stultifying. It was packed with artefacts, all the brightest and best things from the collection, in a jumble that allowed no close examination, with Lord Sisley like a dragon with his hoard. Ibis noted, the way he could not help notice artwork, that much of it was Mesopotamian, including a sizeable mosaic panel depicting the sirrush, the snake-dragon of Marduk, in well-preserved tiles of bright blue and copper-beige.

"You have been doing research about some matter in Norfolk?" The question drew Ibis back to his scolding.

"Yes, sir. An outside consultation."

"Tell me about it."

Ibis considered, in the moment he had. What should he say and what should he avoid?

"Sir," he began. "It is a consultation for a widow of scholarly interests. Her husband was a research fellow here before the War, Octavian Gates. A good family, well known in Hampshire." He hoped the names protect in some way, if he used the soothing syllables, the names that were all about a green and gentle England, not whatever fancies people had about what Ibis did. Or who he was.

Lord Sisley gave nothing away. "Her name?"

"Proserpina Gates, sir. Her maiden name was Lewis. I gather her father is fairly high in the Indian Colonial Service, the magical side, of course." He hated to go this route, but he was sure with Sisley that it was the only way through.

"Not a family I know well." That earned a little snort. "I'll ask the wife."

Ibis nodded. "A widow, sir, taking on research projects to supplement her business, which is a bookstore."

"What is your role, then?" Lord Sisley's voice was curt.

"She wrote for an appointment before Christmas last year, and when she arrived, no one had scheduled her. I was in my office, so Davis sent her up to me." That was phrased to avoid mentioning he'd been the only one in the building.

"That was January, wasn't it?"

"The fourteenth, sir."

"It is now late March."

"Yes, sir."

"You have other things to fill your time, surely?"

"Sir, my recent reports mention that at the moment, while the excavation season is ongoing in Egypt, I have limited access to the collection. I expect the various excavators to return in the next two to six weeks, and will again be able to continue with my project. In the meantime, I am a little at loose ends, having completed my work with the available material at the beginning of February."

"What did Mrs Gates ask you to assist with?"

"Mrs Gates had been working with someone who lives somewhat near her, to identify whether there might be a lost Roman hoard on the family estate in East Anglia."

"Where precisely?"

"Near Norfolk, sir." He couldn't lie, it was far too easy for someone to check.

"What did you learn on the initial consultation?"

"Mrs Gates laid out the research she had done. She was not sure what the next step was, what kind of specialist would be of most use. An archaeologist, a linguist, a materia specialist, something else."

Lord Sisley nodded. "I will grant you have some experience that might be relevant."

Ibis bit the inside of his lip, enough to hold back the

comments he wanted to make. He was old enough to know how much worse that would make everything.

"Sir. I pointed out that my skills were an interesting fit with her needs. Her Middle English is much better than mine, but the Latin is well within my skills, even given some dialect issues, and the archaeological questions are quite interesting."

That earned him the miniscule praise of a raised eyebrow, showing actual interest.

"Of course, sir, most of my experience is in arid climates, or those that flood seasonally, rather than England, but there are signs that a change in the river course may have affected how the possible locations for the hoard appeared over time. Close reading of the available documents so far shows they shifted in ways that would not be predicted by current understanding."

"A geological cause, do you think, or magical?"

"It is impossible to say for certain, sir, without further study and evaluation. I would say both are plausible, but given the rumours about the hoard, one cannot rule out magical influence." He disliked being so specific, but he had to say something, offer some crumb of possibility. All of this about the river was true and inarguable.

"What work have you done so far?"

"Mrs Gates has sent copies of material for me to translate, we have collaborated through correspondence and two meetings here. She arranged for me to visit her client's home and look at the records there. The materials bear out cause to support significant investigation. Mrs Gates has handled all the details. As of last night, my logged time on this project is twenty-three hours over three months, including travel time."

"Does that include your Saturday?" Lord Sisley's voice turned sharp.

"Yes, sir." He wouldn't duck it. Clearly, that would be a stupid and foolish direction to go. Sisley had to have some reason for calling him in, and the most logical one had to do with the events of Saturday. But beyond that, this kind of lie always tripped one up later. Learning that young had kept him alive before this, and he would have to trust it would again.

"Tell me about Saturday."

"That was my decision, sir. I did not discuss it with Mrs Gates in advance. I have the habit, as you may remember me mentioning, sir, of taking a portal to a suitable location for a good country walk on a Saturday I do not have other obligations."

Ibis paused for breath, then continued, "I do not know Norfolk well, but as it is spring, and there were several public paths, I thought I might contribute to the research by better understanding the landscape. I brought the usual Ordnance Survey maps, my walking stick, a packed lunch, as is my habit."

"What did you do?" Lord Sisley leaned forward a little. Ibis was suddenly glad that whatever else this man was, and whatever power he might abuse, he clearly had not been Intelligence in the War, and clearly discounted such modern innovations as learning to read body language.

The slight shift in how he was leaning was one thing, but the way his eyes widened, how the muscles of his face had gone still, all of them were very informative. He was entirely confident in his power now. Which made him, perhaps, less of a threat. Perhaps. Sisley moved his hand slightly, and Ibis caught a flash of a coppery colour from a ring.

"Portal to Norwich, and then a short walk to the site. I stayed entirely on public paths, sir, they were well marked." This was where he would have to be very careful. He kept his voice even, pleasantly neutral, as if there was no danger here. Even thought there was.

"What happened, from your point of view."

"I was approached by two people on the path, saying I was trespassing, and should get out. They used distasteful language, sir, but made themselves quite clear." It had been long enough since he'd been on the knife edge of this kind of interrogation he had to focus on keeping his breath even, avoiding the tells of nervousness. His mentor in the Great Game had drilled him and drilled him until it was instinct, and yet it almost wasn't enough.

"Did you give any cause for trouble?"

"No, sir. I left as quickly as they permitted."

"That is not what I heard from the Caistor St Edmund Guard." That sentence, so simple, was so menacing. Ibis prevented himself from responding in the more obvious ways, at least, and then had to figure out what one said to that.

"Sir, I am glad to make appropriate oath as to what occurred."

He didn't want to. He was afraid anyone who took his oath would keep asking questions, and some of those might be dangerous too. But the offer of the oath is the instinctive thing for an honest British man of magic, so it was the only thing he could do.

This earned him another raised eyebrow.

"You were educated at Schola, yes?"

It was in his file, and it's not like anyone would let him in here without that. They both knew it. "Yes, sir. Seal House."

That earned him another slight nod.

"Do not go near Norwich again without explicit permission from the landowner. And sufficient advance warning to the Guard, to avoid trouble. Your regular project resumes in April, you said?"

"It depends when the professors return, sir, but April or early May at the latest."

"You will write me weekly updates, with a full log of your time." The thing one demanded of a first year apprentice, who had not yet proven they could manage the adult world. Demeaning, and everyone would know it, too, because he'd have to turn the thing in on Friday at noon when people made note of who was in the office and what they were doing.

"As you like, sir." He kept his tone light.

"If you need more to keep you busy, I'm sure we can hunt out something that needs indexing." Again, apprentice work. Necessary and useful, but not what Ibis was here for.

"Sir, I will let you know."

Just like that, there was a wave of the hand. "Report on Friday, then." There was a hint that he'd nearly tacked on 'boy' and had managed not to.

Ibis stood, made the polite inclined bow, again, and murmured, "Sir. Happy Monday, sir."

He made it back to his office in the attics. He managed to trigger the privacy charms before he entirely lost his temper and had to spend five minutes swearing profusely - and rather inventively, by the end of it - in Arabic to calm down.

"Bad day?"

Ibis was halfway through a beer, sitting on their sofa, staring vaguely at his shrine. He'd heard Jonas on the stairs, but hadn't moved to get a beer or any of the other sociable things he ought to do. Jonas came around and peered at him while taking off his coat.

"Sisley called me in."

Jonas blinked and then said, "Let me get a beer, then." He disappeared into his room and came back out in shirt-sleeves with his cuffs and collar loosened. He ducked into the kitchen space to grab a beer before he came back and sat down in the facing chair.

"Sisley's head of everything, right?"

"Lord Sisley, technically. Yes. Chief Scholar of the Research Society."

"You forget, my friend, I am an upstart American, with no appreciation for titles. What does that mean in reality?" There was a hint of something under Jonas's voice, and Ibis couldn't help recognising that Jonas had had another round of status games in his day. He often did.

It was enough to make him look up and soften. "This is queer even for England, so you're not missing much."

Jonas snorted and took a long sip of his beer. "Go on, then."

"I gave you the speech about how Father was a local landowner, but not a lord, not one of the people responsible for the land in a particular way, didn't I? With the part about how it is not just about land, but sometimes other responsibilities, magically speaking."

"It was arcane balderdash that I suppose makes sense to people here, but seems entirely foolish to me. You explained it though." Jonas was at least amiable about the local oddities so long as no one expected him to do anything about the foolishness.

"Lord Sisley is in his - oh, must be late sixties, maybe early seventies by now. That ageless older man look magical folk get. He's still quite active, physically and mentally, and he thinks he's on top of the world."

Jonas drawled, "Well, by his lights he is. Power, money. White, I presume, though I can't always tell with you lot."

Ibis nodded, absentmindedly, then was struck by a distracting thought, and Jonas raised an eyebrow. "Just realised something," Ibis said. "I'll come back to it."

Jonas nodded. "So why did Sisley call you in? Last I heard, you had a peaceful weekend in mind. Sorry I wasn't here, assume you got my note." They had called him in to cover multiple shifts at the hospital. They did that, when the people who should have the midnight shifts had some fancy party they'd rather be at.

"I did. I went up walking. In Norfolk."

"Near your hoard?"

"That was the idea." Ibis's tone turned dry as sawdust.

"It didn't go off as planned?"

"I found the land easily enough. And then I got run off by a pair - one of them had a shotgun, and a mouth on him. Nothing as inventive as my uncles, but you can't have every-thing." He tried to pass it off.

"That bad, mm?" Mind, passing it off never worked with Jonas. He knew what Ibis was hiding, for the same reasons Ibis could see through Jonas not mentioning the daily slings and arrows.

"I got off without being shot."

"That does not define a particularly good day. What did you do?"

"Train and a rickety community bus and a walk in the rain to True Eyeworth."

"You could have come back here. Come round the hospital." And then Jonas caught something and leaned forward. "Did they hurt you?" It was suddenly intense.

Ibis flushed. "He hit me. That's when I ran. I don't think he expected me to be that fast."

"You've got a bruise left over your eye. Gone yellow enough it's hard to see with your skin tone." And then what Ibis expected. "You tried to hurry it, didn't you?"

"I didn't have a choice, and you know it." Turning up with a visible bruise was a trouble he couldn't talk his way out of.

"Hmm. Well. We're pausing your storytelling for me to fix that. Five minutes, I need to dig up the right salve to support it. You go have a wash, change into something comfortable."

"How about I do a plate for supper. Nothing fancy, but there are sandwich makings..."

"Won't turn that down. Fifteen minutes, then."

They separated, and Ibis could hear Jonas muttering from his room as he hunted in the various apothecary drawers where he stashed things. Ten minutes later, Ibis had washed, changed into his dressing gown, and set out a carving board. They'd had more than he'd thought, and there was ham, cheese, bread, and the pot of good mustard, along with the last of the pickles.

"There. Right. You sit on the couch here, I have the salve. Turn your head here, so I can get a good look in the light."

Jonas was very sure with his hands. They'd done this a few times now, when Ibis took some bruise or other more physical mark of people's dislike. Ibis closed his eyes, letting Jonas work his thumb and the salve across the bruise.

"You got lucky. It would have been nasty, a bit to the right. We can't mend eyes."

Ibis winced, and something about Jonas being so matter-of-fact brought it home. "Tried to duck."

Jonas snorted and kept on with his work. Ibis could feel the magic flowing through it now, easing the bruising and swelling.

"Anywhere else? Anything pulled?"

"Nothing some stretching and a hot bath didn't fix."

Jonas nodded and gestured for Ibis to go on.

"There was this thing..." He shook his head, picking up the story. "I went to Pross because I was scared they'd track her down, she needed to know."

"And you couldn't send a note in that journal of yours?"

"It seemed rude. 'Pardon, sorry, I've put you at some risk without discussing it in advance, hope you don't mind awfully.'" His voice got very English, and Jonas laughed.

"Point."

"It was a long trek. And when I got there, someone - turned out to be her daughter - opened the door. She must look a bit like her father. Mother around the face, but.." Ibis opened his eyes, Jonas had finished with the touching. "I suspect her father was black, or at least mixed. Something about the hair and the skin tone."

He was cautious, saying this, but Jonas nodded. "Not that uncommon here. Even among the well-off families, I gather. That's why my family wanted me to study the magical side, not the physical."

"And yet you refused."

Jonas shrugged. "I know as much of the magical as I need for right now. Go on, so you saw her daughter."

"Cammie. She closed the door on me. And then she handed me an umbrella. But she at least told her mother, and there was an apology by way of hot cocoa."

Jonas laughed. "There are worse."

"And Pross sat me down, and gave me this thing in a foot bath. I wonder if she'll share the recipe, it felt amazing. Mint and something else, and a fair pinch of something magical." He was rambling, but even the memory made him feel that surge of relief, that he wasn't on his own.

"Mint's good for sore feet. Mama's salve has some, I'll make you more. But if you get that recipe, I'll try it."

Ibis nodded, then continued. "She insisted on putting me up for the night, once I explained what happened. Wouldn't hear of it otherwise. And she..."

Jonas tilted his head, then said, "She what?"

"She was just... it was safe there. Even though I'd gone there because I was afraid she might get hurt. And it, I turned up in the middle of a storm, after dark, when her daughter was home, and."

Jonas nodded. "And then you came back here?"

"The next day, the portal she knows, the lord there. Much more sensible sort than Sisley, I must say."

"And then Sisley called you in?"

"He did. And it was all him showing his power. He insisted I answer for what I'd done, which is well within my autonomy, and besides which I'd gone on my own time, and now he wants weekly reports." It came out in a rush.

"Implying, of course, you can't manage your own work. Like a child."

Ibis nodded and shook his head. "And it was more jarring, because..." He let his voice trail off.

"Because?"

"She took care of me. Saw to me. The first thing she asked after I said they'd hit me was asking if I was all right."

Jonas was about to say something, but then said, "Go on?"

"I didn't expect Sisley to care, but I expected him to ask. And he didn't even go into it." He paused, then said, "In hindsight, like he knew I wasn't hurt. Or not badly." Ibis frowned. "He'd heard the details from them, I'm sure of it. How did they know to tell him?"

Jonas nodded, and then said, "You do realise you're sweet on this woman, right?"

Ibis looked up, sharply. "I'm not. She's just. She's sensible."

"And you went running to her in the pouring rain when you were hurt and in shock, she took you in, and she treated you like the decent thoughtful person you are. That's all too rare in this world."

Ibis blinked. And blinked again. And then he buried his face in his hands. "And I just asked her to go to Paris with me."

EIGHTEEN

PARIS

"Why am I meeting you in Paris?"

Pross felt like she had moved heaven and earth to turn up in the Grand Salle des Portes by nine on Wednesday morning, and then she had seen no sign of Ibis for a good half hour. An inquiry informed her that London's portals were backed up by an hour. She had retreated for twenty minutes to acquire coffee and a croissant. She was in Paris, after all.

Now he was here, looking very much in control of himself, and he'd somehow collected a very attentive porter since coming out of the portal. Ibis moved his hand, one of the common gestures of the Intelligence service to show the need for discretion. She caught the quick brush of two fingers over the wrist, like you were adjusting a watch. She nodded and followed his lead.

"The library has an interesting exhibit, and materials relevant to our interests. Is that your bag? I made arrangements at the Hotel D'Anjou."

She blinked. "Out of my usual price range," she said, carefully. "And my client's."

"All taken care of, a friend of my family's owed me a favour. Your own room, of course."

This was not at all what she expected, and she did a quick evaluation. He'd warned her, by journal, to bring a nice dress as well as daytime clothing, but she'd assumed it was for a meeting with someone, not staying at one of the better magical hotels in the city. Perhaps she could pick up a silk scarf or something of the kind to go over the dress, which suited her well, but was not quite up to snuff for a fashionable dinner out.

No helping it now, she could sort it out later. "Lead on, then, m'sieur." He murmured to the porter, a quick flurry of French asking him to find a carriage, and see to Pross's bag and his own case.

Fifteen minutes later, they checked into the hotel. Ibis murmured, "Twenty minutes to freshen up? Research this afternoon, we'll come back and change for the evening." She nodded, and spent the time tidying her hair and extracting the deep purple cloche hat she had brought on a whim, and which matched the trim on her spring coat.

She was ready a good five minutes before Ibis knocked, presenting an arm to escort her in a rather more formal show of manners than she was used to. He looked inherently more European, wearing a dark grey jacket that fit him beautifully, and with a puff of deep blue silk tucked impeccably into the top of his waistcoat. If she had seen him on the street, she could easily not have matched him up with the drab London scholar.

She raised an eyebrow at him, but he made it clear it was not yet time for explanations. "I thought we might walk down the river, to the library, if you don't mind? It's about twenty minutes from here, but quite lovely in spring." He glanced at her feet, but she was wearing comfortable enough shoes, and so she nodded.

They spent the first ten minutes of the walk in amiable conversation, like they were friends enjoying the city. Pross noticed that he was very attentive to their surroundings, pausing several times to let people behind them pass, directing her attention to a window or historical building, and generally keeping good space between them and the others on the sidewalk.

She wondered, fleetingly, if anyone thought they were more than friends, but then he said something about one building along the river. She was distracted by his explanation of how the river shaped things differently here than in London or Alexandria.

When they had just passed the Cathedral of Notre Dame, he drew her into a small park along the river, and checking they were not overheard, then pulling out a pocket watch and studying it closely. "There. Private enough." he said.

"For an explanation?"

Ibis nodded, turning to her, and looking serious. "Tell me if you see anyone. Or anything unusual."

She nodded, suddenly concerned. "You're taking several precautions. Is there a particular reason?"

"Half a dozen, but I am fairly sure none of them will be looking for us in Paris."

"There is that." She tried to make it light-hearted, but it came out edged.

He looked abashed. "I didn't even ask, is this all right? Your daughter, I didn't, did I take you away from her?"

"She's with my friend Ferry, for today and tomorrow. She'll have a grand time and ride ponies and play with Ferry's daughter and have a lot to tell me about when I get back. I do need a portal back by about four though. There's a party at the house in the evening, and I don't want her getting underfoot."

Then, daring a bit more openness than she'd been accustomed to, she added, "Mind, Cammie was quite put out I was going to Paris on the spur of the moment. I must find something to bring back for her. And a thank you for Ferry."

Ibis nodded, then visibly spent ten seconds rearranging what he wanted to say. He began with, "I am sorry, I wouldn't have asked if it weren't important."

Pross nodded, and after a moment said, "You have earned a fair bit of trust from me. I will say I'm not quite used to my trusting someone leading to Parisian adventures."

He blushed, dark enough she could see it. "It only seemed fair I make the arrangements. I hope it's all right? The room?"

"Ibis, you've seen my flat. The room is glorious. I may feel insufficiently fashionable at supper, but that is a survivable problem."

Something in her tone must have reassured him because he nodded. "You know what happened Saturday, the relevant parts. I spent Sunday afternoon at home. Monday, Lord Sisley summoned me to his office promptly at half-one. He's..."

"The Chief Scholar, yes. New since the War, isn't he?"

Ibis blinked at her. "I hadn't known that. I thought he'd been around some time."

"Around the Society, yes, but not Chief Scholar. That's recent, the last four years or so. I can check some notes at home. I kept getting the journal, even after..." Her voice trailed off.

Ibis nodded, then continued. "I suppose you know how men like that are, entirely sure they're right, and need not question anything?"

"It has always seemed like abysmal research technique to me. No one's right all the time. You don't improve if you don't ask questions."

Ibis laughed, despite himself. "I hadn't thought of it like that." He paused, then said, "He was very clear with me that if I continued doing what I was doing, my position would be at some risk. Oh, he didn't come out and say it, but the implication was all through. That he could make things very difficult for me. Reassign me to other tasks. Revoke my fellowship."

"Could he? I thought the projects for the fellows were more settled than that?"

"He's the Chief Scholar, he can do anything he can get the others to go along with."

Pross watched his face and then said, "And you don't have friends there. Or allies."

Ibis shook his head, then looked away, nominally toward the river. "No." He paused, a pause she couldn't make sense of. "After I wrote to you, I realised there might be reasons to take more precautions. Sisley clearly knew about my problems in Norwich, and yet he didn't ask if I was all right. I'm sure he didn't care."

"So why are we here?"

"Because I wanted to be far away from them. Because I hope that we won't have anyone listening over our shoulders." He paused and swallowed. "The public reason is that there are those materials here, in the library, those inscriptions we came across about what might be wards. And there are a couple of useful books since we're here."

She waited, but he didn't go on. "But?" she asked after half a minute.

"I wanted somewhere it would be safe to talk. Where I could be sure no one would overhear us. And you said you knew French, is that a problem? Are you angry?" His voice turned suddenly earnest, even a bit anxious.

Pross paused, then reached for his hand, venturing a physical touch, more than she had on Saturday when she handed him things and set out the footbath. "I am here, Ibis. I trusted you had a reason, and I'm here. For the research, and the lovely hotel, and I presume a nice meal or two."

"There's a restaurant," Ibis said, hesitantly. "The hotel really is a favour. My mother has a cousin, he arranged the reservation on short notice."

"What precautions will make you feel better?" Pross wasn't sure she wanted to make him think about that, but he was clearly already worrying about it.

"The usual gestures, though they're not as private as I'd like. We don't have time to sort out individual ones. If you don't mind, French in public? And avoiding discussion of our research when there are other people around? Other than the necessities with the librarian?" He had been thinking about this.

"Certainly. I'm a little rusty speaking, but not too bad, I think. Is the library expecting us?"

"Yes. We'll go in, sort out what we want to see, then take a break for lunch while they fetch it. There's a nice bistro nearby, quite pleasant. Quite a few other researchers."

"Hence the caution." It wasn't a question.

"Yes. You don't mind?"

She shook her head. "Not any of it. I'll follow your lead." She considered. "Maybe spontaneity is good for me?"

NINETEEN

PARIS

Pross felt entirely discombobulated by the time they finished with the library. They retreated to the hotel after taking the third cab to pull up. It felt ridiculous, to go back to the protocols of the Intelligence Service, but there you were. The habits were right under her skin, and Ibis clearly felt the same, from how smoothly he did his part.

Pross suspected he'd seen much more active service than she had, from how he chose a table at the bistro where they could see all the relevant approaches and have at least three exits, and how he'd asked for a quick tour of the research area before they settled down. That wasn't surprising, given all the women she'd known had been discouraged from more active roles.

His approach had been amusing. Once he switched into French he persisted in using the informal with her, switching into a polished professional tone when speaking to others. Pross had been glad to let him do most of the talking.

Ibis seemed quite different, here. She wasn't sure if it

was picking up his Intelligence skills, or being outside of England, or both, but there was something very polished, very self-assured. Like he was taking up more space. She found it compelling. Even, she had to admit to herself, attractive beyond the purely aesthetic appreciation she'd had since he turned up that morning.

A flying research visit was always intense, trying to cram all the things you wanted to find in the records into a few hours. Doing one in her third language was worse, and there was the looming sense of worry about whether people had figured out where Ibis was going. Something in the library itself also felt a little queer to her, a peculiar itching between her shoulders, like someone was watching.

Fussing about how rusty her French might be was at least a distraction while she got ready for the evening. She focused on getting her hair to behave. She'd sent a note to Cammie, hoping to reassure her that everything was fine. At least she could trust that Cammie was quite safe.

The wards at Ytene were excellent, she'd helped with some research about them when Carillon and Lizzie settled in. As Carillon had said, they were both perfectly good scholars, but the Achilles heel of research is that you have your own pet theories, so another set of well-informed eyes would only improve things.

This left her forced to consider the evening. They had indeed found a shop where she could buy a few fripperies - a glorious scarf in amber and deep blue that went with her blue dress, a smaller one for Cammie, and a hat of deep green felted wool she thought Ferry would love. Ibis had said they could talk after supper.

She was just putting the finishing touches on her cosmetics and adjusting the fall of the silk skirt when she heard the knock on the door. It was the quiet rhythm they'd picked, and she tapped the door with the response before opening it. If Ibis had looked good that morning, he looked fantastic now, in full formal dress, his movements as clean and precise as the clothing he wore.

"My!" It slipped out before she could stop herself.

He ducked his head and flushed, then said, "My pleasure. If you're ready, the table should be waiting for us when we get downstairs."

They were eating downstairs, not simply because it was safer, though it was, but because the restaurant at the Hotel D'Anjou was supposed to be spectacular. Their new chef apparently had a grand passion for melding historical recipes with modern approaches. New sauces, using the latest magical techniques to make them smooth as glass, bringing foreign spices in nad melding them with French cheeses and wines and bread. She wished she'd had time to read up on it in advance.

Ibis crooked his arm, to escort her, and they went off to descend the quite imposing stairs. She felt underdressed, even with the scarf, and yet there was something in how Ibis was watching her, steadily, that was tremendously flattering. If she'd been younger, she'd have thought he was almost flirting.

Dinner itself was overwhelming, in all the best ways. They talked, through the meal, mostly about the food, with Ibis lending a hand with vocabulary as she needed it. Her French was of the more practical sort, rather than discussing the nuances of a robust herb sauce that went with lamb, or a citrus sauce with duck. Part way through the main course, he asked, carefully, "Have you travelled much?"

She lit up, she could feel herself glowing. "Oh, yes. Not

as much as I'd like, and not much since the War. But Octavian did his research in Hungary, I've mentioned that, and
we spent a couple of wonderful weeks in Vienna for part of
the same project. Provence one summer, though only a day
or two in Paris, when his parents took a place for the season,
not long after we married. A few short trips, Rome and
Madrid. Entirely in Europe, though. We'd talked about
other places, but then we had Cammie, and then the War,
and ..." She shrugged.

"And India." Ibis was amused.

"Well, yes." Pross paused, then asked. "You?"

"I grew up in Egypt, and we came to England when I
was eleven. After I finished school, Father made sure I had a
Grand Tour, and then they posted me to Egypt for part of
the War."

Pross ventured a question about Egypt, and found Ibis
willing enough to talk about the history, what it was like
growing up in cities that had been large and active for thou-
sands of years. That carried them through the main course,
through the sweet and coffee, and then Ibis murmured,
"Shall we find somewhere to talk? There's a roof garden
that might be quiet enough?"

She nodded, and let him escort her up there, finding a
sheltered bench that had a gorgeous view of the lights of the
city intertwining with the dark ribbon of the river. She
closed her eyes in sheer pleasure, and when she opened
them, he was close, watching her, leaning in slightly.

Pross suddenly wanted to kiss him, very badly, the
desire overtaking her good sense in a rush. He was a
colleague. She had had no sign, other than that moment in
the bookshop, that he might welcome anything further. And
yet, here she was, in her best dress, and a new scarf, and
with the afterglow of an amazing meal. And here he was,

handsome and taking up space, and confident. It might just be Paris, but she thought it was more than that.

She could not resist, and like a dive into a pool of clear water, she reached to touch his cheek, then she leaned in. There was a moment of hesitation, giving him enough space to pull away, to discourage her. He didn't. She kissed him, taking her time with it, not a friendly peck on the cheek, but something much more vulnerable.

Perhaps it surprised him. Almost immediately, though, his hand came up to cup her cheek, steady himself, and return the kiss. He did not press, he did not take charge, but instead let it be a dance or perhaps a song. Not leading, not following, but the different voice parts twining and making something new.

Neither of them wanted to pull away, and it was only when she needed breath that she could think of stopping. She felt the brush of his thumb, then she was blinking, trying to make her eyes focus on him, trying to read his reaction, which was hopeless at the best of times.

"Are you, did..." The words stuttered, as he looked back at her. She could not sort out his expression at all.

"I - that." She stopped. She sounded like a fool.

Which left them staring at each other in silence, in the shadows, lit only by the faint lights from the surrounding buildings. Suddenly, she shivered, and he said, "Oh, you must be cold. Should I, should we?"

Pross couldn't decide what to do with this. Did he want to stop? Was he suggesting something else?

While she was dithering, he stood up, and offered his hands. "Come, please. Come back inside. I'll walk you down to your room. It's been a very long day for us both. We can talk about the project in the morning."

She was not at all sure what she thought about that.

When she stood up, it was clear that the wine she'd had with dinner was rushing through her head, and she was more unsteady than she would like to admit. Eventually she nodded, and took his arm, and let him walk her back downstairs.

TWENTY

PARIS

I bis woke the next morning with a pounding headache. It was not the wine that had got him, so much as being up well past two trying to figure out what was happening with his life.

He had enjoyed the kiss, but it had thrown him into turmoil. Did she really want to kiss him? Did she mean it? Or was it the wine and the food and the beauty of Paris that had made her lose her mind?

The dream he'd woken from hadn't helped at all, of kissing her, up against a wall, much like his sitting room, of taking her to his bedroom. He couldn't imagine that happening in reality, and yet the dreaming meant he felt like he almost could reach out and touch it, if he were only to presume.

The knock at the door came again. That would be the breakfast he'd arranged for both of them after he'd taken her down to her room. It would give her a chance to regroup, to settle herself. It would give him a chance to wake up.

He found his dressing gown, and came to the door, checking and making sure it was only the waiter he'd expected. He pressed a small gratuity into the man's hand, heard the murmur that he'd seen to the lady already, and that the private sitting room they'd arranged would be ready in an hour.

Ibis ate, barely tasting what was a perfectly good breakfast, before washing and changing. Then finally, he had to go down and see what the state of the baffling world was, though he was not so bewildered that he forgot to take the usual precautions for safety. When he knocked on Pross's door, she opened it up immediately after giving the proper response. She looked both very fetching - hair softly pinned up - and restrained, in a high-necked blouse and skirt.

"Last night, I -" She stopped, and then said, "You know, that sounded better in my head."

Ibis had to smile. Something about her made it impossible to stay too nervous. "Please, Pross. I enjoy working with you, and there's no need to make this awkward. We had rather a complicated day yesterday, and Paris does has a reputation."

She smiled at that, but then sobered. "I - it was not kind of me. I don't know what it is you..." She stopped, then started again. "We haven't talked at all about how either of us views relationships, or might, beyond a little about my late husband. I shouldn't have kissed first, without some more conversation."

"Even if I enjoyed it?" Ibis couldn't resist asking. His self-control was better than this, damn it. It had to be. It ought to be.

"Especially if you enjoyed it." Her voice got softer, and she looked away for a moment, down toward the floor.

He reached for her hand, and said, "We can talk more about it, if you'd like. Though perhaps not today. Let us both sleep on it. Perhaps write about some of it if that would be easier for you?"

"Would it be easier for you?"

"Being able to look at what's written and revise it is... yes." He blushed. "I admit it's often easier."

She nodded. "Then let's do that. What is the plan for today?" She felt relived he was willing to table the question for now.

"You needed to be back through the portal by four. I made reservations for you at three, and me at half-three. Until, then, there's a private sitting room we can use here, with a table."

"No more library?"

He shook his head. "Unless you've thought of something else we should see?"

Pross half-closed her eyes. "Something felt peculiar there. I'm not sure what. It might just be a different style of indexing magics, or protective charms or something of the kind." She paused, then ventured, "It made that spot between my shoulders itch."

"And you are a woman who trusts your instincts." He wondered if she had picked up on his interest in her, if he'd given any hint, to provoke that kiss, and it made the sentence come out more flatly than he'd intended.

His tone was apparently noncommittal enough she opened her eyes, looking at him more sharply. "You didn't feel anything?"

"No, I did. Nothing significant enough to leave, but ... something just a hair off. Again, it could be nothing to do with us."

"So we'll take precautions. I presume that means we're not going out to lunch?"

"No, we'll eat here. If you hand me your case, I can take

it for you. They'll bring us lunch." That, at least, was a thing he could do, a courtesy where they both knew how it went.

"Thank you for arranging breakfast, it was just the thing." She blushed again. "As it gave me time to figure out what to say to you."

Ibis had to smile, and try to reassure her. "We should talk more, when we've had time to sort out what we want to say. Both of us. But I'm not upset with you. A little startled, but not upset at all."

"You didn't think me inclined to do that?"

"Proserpina, you have shown me your patience and practicality so far in our acquaintanceship, not your spontaneity."

That made her laugh, and then she said, "I came and meet you in Paris on barely any notice. Also, I think we might might call this friendship now."

"There is that." He then held out his hand. "Come along, let's get settled in and look at our notes from yesterday."

The process of setting out their notes was reassuring. They both had established habits about it, and their habits fit well together. He had a particular way of setting out his pen and ink, his pencils. She preferred to deal with the written materials first.

This time, she brought out an ingenious folding wooden stand that held them at a comfortable angle. He brushed his fingers over it once she sat down. "This is lovely."

Pross looked up, smiling. "It is very useful. It was a gift from Mistress Howell, the woman I apprenticed with. She had an eye for what she called practical beauty."

He considered this. "Can you explain?"

Pross waved a hand. "She loved books. You know how some people love books for what they hold, and some people love books for the beauty of the object? She loved all the books, forever, but she loved them in different ways. The gorgeous incunabulum and the scruffiest chapbook, turning into pulp in your hands."

Ibis settled into the chair beside Pross, thinking about that. "That's a very specific attitude."

Pross nodded. "She felt so strongly about connecting people with the right book for them, in that moment. That it was an act of matchmaking, a glorious magic that you couldn't force. She insisted that when you got it right, it was like nothing in the world."

Ibis hesitated, and then he couldn't resist, she brought him to the edge of the precipice again entirely differently. "If you were to hand me a book, what would you hand me?"

She settled back, but he got the sense that it was so she could look at more of him, not just his face or his hands. "There's a book...." As if she was deciding what to risk.

He waited, barely breathing. This was the most intimate moment he'd had in years, waiting to understand what she saw of him.

"I'm not sure you'd like it. But I think you'd find it worth reading." She decided, visibly, and went ahead. "It's a curious book, set in different rooms of the same building, over decades, centuries. Abigail Loren's *Threshold*. Each story is a different room, a different time, a different set of people. Some of them are more successful as tales than others, but when you fit the pieces together, it's ..."

She waved a hand. "It's like being in a cathedral, the colours of the stained glass all over, the light so amazing, and all the details of the carvings and the woodwork and how they designed the floor, all coming together. You could read it a hundred times and find something new."

Ibis let out his breath. "And you think that is the book for me?"

"You would appreciate it." Pross hesitated for just a moment more and then said, "One character reminds me of you. Guarded, but with excellent reason. Fiercely intelligent, and yet so used to not letting it show. Again, with good reason."

That was so sharply correct that Ibis had to turn away, and cough, anything to break the mood a little. When he turned back, he said, "I would like to read it. Will you send me a copy? I can send you the coin."

Pross smiled, suddenly relaxed and at ease, as if there had been some test he had not even known he was taking, perhaps one she had not realised she was setting him. "Oh, you arranged a lovely night, I think I can offer you the book in exchange."

He smiled back, and then stood, moving to wash his hands in the attached lavatory before handling their more delicate notes. "Where should we begin, then? Make the most of our time?"

"What do you think this hoard is?" The question seemed to come out of nowhere, but Ibis had the sense she'd been working around to it for a while.

"I showed you the summaries of the hoards found so far. Coins, jewellery, perhaps a plate or cup or something of the kind."

"That's…" She paused, rummaging for words.

He didn't rush her, just shifted to listen, to focus on her.

"That makes little sense. Why chase you off? Why get worried you might find something? What is it that Lord Sisley is protecting?"

"You're certain he's protecting something?"

"Something. Someone. Maybe several someones."

"Do you think it's something in the hoard? How would they know about it?"

Pross waved a hand. "The old families, the Great Families, they share information with their own. They always have, always will, from before the waves drowned Ys until the sun goes cold." It had the ring of a ritual phrase for her.

"Your family?" He asked cautiously, not sure what he wanted the answer to be.

"The more distant parts, yes. Enough of them."

"Can you help me navigate, then?"

Pross looked at him, quiet, as if she was trying to read him like a manuscript. Perhaps a faded and worn one, the way she kept searching for something specific. After nearly a minute, she nodded, and said, "I'll do my best."

TWENTY-ONE

LONDON

Something was up. Ibis could feel it in every bone in his spine and hair on the back of his neck. And yet, he could do nothing but go about the day they expected him to have, do the tasks they expected him to do.

He was almost onto the staircase, aiming for the relative safety it offered, when he heard the leather-soled shoes behind him, the slight squeak he couldn't help but identify.

"Ward, old man."

Ibis turned, and offered the appropriate smile for the occasion, the one that was all pleasant cordiality. "Aimtree."

"You weren't in the office yesterday. Any reason?"

It was sharper than Ibis had expected, and he shifted his body to avoid all the tells of his discomfort. Or at least, all the ones he could control. "Investigating a few questions," he said, evenly.

"I heard you had a bit of difficulty with Lord Sisley." Aimtree's tone turned confiding.

"Did you?" Ibis kept his tone light.

"Look, old man, I could make things easier for you."

Ibis was entirely sure that was not true. Or rather, it

could be true for a certain kind of man, and Ibis wanted nothing to do with that person. That sort of man would be someone who bent his ethics to suit the situation, or worse.

"I'm quite happy with my research, other than the current scheduling holdup, thanks awfully." It was amazing how throwing in a phrase or two, in the right accent, often defused things. The more he could remind people like Aimtree that he was just as English as he was Egyptian, the better, in his experience.

"Look, come along to my office for a moment, would you?"

It was the last thing Ibis wanted. On the other hand, refusing would be seen not only as rude and distrustful, but be a salvo in this skirmish that might grow into something much larger.

"I have a few minutes, Aimtree. Certainly. Do lead on."

He couldn't tell, but he thought Aimtree seemed put out that he didn't object or demur.

When they got to Aimtree's office, Ibis was struck by the difference from his own. It wasn't just the amount of room and the location, though those were splendid. Aimtree had a prime view to the square, large windows, good light.

More than that, the furniture and artwork was lovely. He thought the chaise in the back was striking. Ornate and rather too red for his tastes, but of high quality, and with beautiful lines of wood carving, evoking something Assyrian or Babylonian, perhaps.

There were books on the shelves. Ibis couldn't help noticing that several of them were volumes he'd searched for and been unable to find in the Society's library on the ground floor. And they were not at all relevant to Aimtree's public research interests. Half a dozen paintings hung on the walls, very much in the ornate and chaotic display of the late 1800s, all scenes set in massive sandstone buildings and marble palaces.

"Have a seat." Aimtree gestured at a decidedly less comfortable chair and settled on the chaise. His tone was much more order than request.

Ibis sat, taking the path of going along to see what Aimtree was up to.

"Old fellow, you must understand we just want you to fit in properly. Sisley's a good sort, but I'd be shocked if he weren't a bit concerned. You disappearing, what if something had happened?"

"Oh, people would have noticed. I share rooms with a medical student, and while he has an odd schedule, he pays attention if I don't turn up when expected."

This was visibly news to Aimtree, and a series of expressions flickered across his face. It was a mix of distaste and startlement and perhaps a morsel of guilt that made Ibis wonder.

"That must be rather dire, having to share. I had quite enough of that at school."

Ibis shrugged, keeping his reply light and genial. "It's handy to have someone bring in the mail and water the plants when I travel for work. When I started here, I was back and forth to Egypt several times, you might remember."

"Never been out of the country, myself." Aimtree said, as if he were proud of it.

"Even in the War?"

"I served in Trellech, handling reports, and then here in London, a promotion, coordinating services."

It made Ibis suspect that someone had indeed pulled strings to keep Aimtree out of the War, given how defensive he was about it. He also noticed Aimtree didn't ask about his own service, which tended to mark those who were insecure about their own.

"Ah. Well, it is handy to have someone to keep an eye on the place. Was there something you needed while I was out?"

"Lord Sisley is very set on making the Research Society move forward properly. He feels that the former role of the society was often rather limited in scope, being too attentive to minute details that were not strictly necessary."

Ibis refused to let his reaction show, managing a pleasant "Oh, do go on?" rather than the paragraphs of lecture that formed in his head. Researchers should be thorough and precise, that was part of the point, and especially so if working with materials that could not easily be rechecked.

"Modernisation, there's the thing. Taking on questions of current interest. I suppose there is some in your projects."

"Egyptology and archaeology do have rather a lot of popular interest, yes. Some of it a tad misguided, I admit, but that is cause for more information, rather than less."

"All those comments about curses and mummies, I suppose. See, that's just the sort of thing Lord Sisley means. Too tied to the past, and too many ridiculous superstitions."

"Ah." Ibis wasn't quite sure where to go with that. "Well, if that's the direction he wishes to take, then I am sure the Society will follow."

"Will you?" Aimtree leaned forward, rather more blunt than Ibis had expected. Ibis had a sudden flash, like lightning, of an impression of scales on rock, and sharp fangs, and a sudden murmur of sound in his ears, rising and then fading away.

He forced himself to take a breath, to stay relaxed, "My skills are mostly with a particular area, I admit. But if Lord

Sisley prefers other directions, I will of course, see what my options are."

It was an unsatisfying answer, and Aimtree clearly thought it insufficient. "I'm sounding out your loyalty, Ward. To be quite blunt."

He hated being pinned down like this. It was taking all of his training, all of his long practice with smaller slings and arrows, to keep himself patient and pleasant.

"Oh, I'm rather a stick in the mud a lot of ways. Before I give my word, I want to know the details. I'm the sort who reads all the pages of a legal document. Bane of anyone who wants to get things done quickly, I'm sure. But I would be glad to hear Lord Sisley or the rest of the Board out. And of course to take my leave at the end of the fellowship if my work no longer suited." There, he could at least remind Aimtree that there were contracts in place, for all the good it would do.

Aimtree paused, then said, "You're queer, Ward. I would have thought someone of your background would have been more aware of the need to find support wherever you could."

Ibis tilted his head. It was the same dance again, the suggestion that things would be easier if he were a little less rigid, a little more flexible in his standards or morals. A little more like them in all the ways they thought mattered.

"I'm grateful for the opportunity to work with the Petrie collection, and for the Society for making that study easier, of course. But I admit I am rather focused on my research, not the social politics. I've never been as good at them as I would like."

That was entirely true. On a bad day, Ibis was in the top fifth or so, when it came to social politics. But he would be much happier to be best at them, or at least best in his particular sphere. Aimtree snorted. "Well, if that's how you are about it, I suppose we know where we stand."

He paused, and Ibis thought he might be dismissed, then Aimtree said, "How's your widow?"

That hit closer to home. "That research is going along well. She's done much of the work, of course."

"Was your trip anything to do with that?" The question was casual, but phrased so that it would be easy to tell a lie.

"A bit, yes. A particular manuscript we thought might have some information. She's still working through the translations, I don't know if there's much in it yet."

"She seemed quite attractive. I looked up her husband, he was quite well regarded. From an excellent family, of course, and her family is in the Great Book, though I gather she's in a cadet branch or something."

"Her father's in the Colonial Service, so there may not be too much recent in the way of updates."

"Ah." It was a very judging sound. "I suppose she developed some tastes young."

The way Aimtree said it, like it was something profane, almost turned the growing interest he had in Pross to ashes, and yet he could not, would not, permit that.

"Scarcely gentlemanly to comment on a woman of good family, surely?" he said after a moment. "I should be getting along. I've an appointment at the Petrie collection in half an hour, and I need to collect my notes." Leaving no space for disagreement, he stood up, and made his way to the door.

TWENTY-TWO

SCHOLA

"Why am I meeting you on Schola?"

Pross was baffled. First Paris. Then the complexities of Paris. And now, here he was again, asking her to meet him.

Here she was, doing what he asked. She wasn't sure why, only she knew that she would of course, meet him where and when he told her.

This time, meeting him involved taking the portal to Schola, and walking down to the village to find the tea shop with the best scones. The walk did not improve her sense of control over her world, but instead left her feeling even more unsettled and uncertain of what she wanted. Did she prefer Ibis to be all business? Or to talk about her impulsiveness?

Ibis stood as she came into the private room he'd reserved, grinning broadly. There was something boyish about him, as if he'd shed a dozen years coming back here.

"Because we met in Paris already this week?" He was in a mood she'd never seen him in before, giddy and all smiles. She had no idea how to answer that, so instead started with a different question. One with an easier answer.

"A pleasant lunch with your sister?" she asked, before considering her answer to the question about Paris. If he was teasing her about it, perhaps he was not upset by her impulsiveness? She watched him, enjoying how he was smiling, feeling tempted to reach out and touch his hand.

"Very, yes. She's doing very well." The pleasure he took in that was just as obvious. "It's grand to see you," he added. "Do, sit, and we can order as soon as you're ready. Master Hase said he'll be free at half-six, so we've a bit of time to sort ourselves out first."

She realised he was waiting for her to sit, so he could push in her chair, and the courtesy delighted her. It was how they'd been in Paris, that edge of flirtation, rather than purely treating each other as professional peers.

"That includes an explanation for why we're here, I hope?" Her voice cracked at the last two words, her roiling emotions getting the better of her.

Ibis obliged immediately, settling into his own chair. "Because I need his advice. I want you there to ask excellent questions I won't think of, and he doesn't leave the island during term."

She took a moment to make sense of the answer, but his sincerity was indeed flattering. She couldn't stop herself from returning a small smile before she said, "That means you need to tell me why you're so insistent about asking."

Someone came to take their orders, interrupting what she might say next. She murmured, "You have a sense of my tastes and know what's good here." That earned her another delighted smile, the corners of his eyes crinkling with it, and he ordered several specific scones and, to her surprise, a proper chai blend.

"It's excellent here, not under spiced. and I thought you might miss the taste."

"I do, but it's not usually in my budget to keep half the spices in the house. Not for tea. They go much further for baking."

Ibis paused, as if he was trying to decide whether to say something, then he offered, "You're cautious about your finances. But not so much you don't enjoy a few luxuries. I like that."

Pross blinked. "Why in particular?"

"Many people, when they're feeling scarcity, they either toss up their hands and spend whatever they have, letting the coin run like water through their fingers. Or they squirrel it away and never spend anything they don't abso- lutely have to. Both have their dangers, and I think they - diminish someone, over time. Someone like you, who will spend a little, in balance, that..." He gestures. "There's breath in that. And breath is magic."

This wasn't at all what she'd expected, and she nodded, thinking hard, before she said anything. "And you like that breath."

"I do, yes." It was very open, very honest.

"You're different here." She hadn't meant to be that blunt, but it was true, and it was important, and somehow, everything in her felt it needed saying.

He blinked, then visibly considered that, what it meant, rather than immediately agreeing or denying it. "I suppose I am. I feel..." He took a breath, settling back in his chair. "I feel safe here, I suppose, in a way I don't most other places. At least as an adult." His gestures were broader, his body relaxed.

"Did you enjoy your time here?" It seemed to her like the obvious question, given his reaction to being here again.

From the way his eyes widened, it was not the one he was expecting.

"Some of it was horrid. Young men can be awful to each other. Young women, I'm sure, too. But the chance to learn things, the chance to explore. My father gave me a lot of choice, far more than many people get, and encouraged me to find what I was particularly good at." That answer, again, was visibly sincere.

"And Master Hase?"

"We weren't close when I was at school, not the way he was with some people. The way all the heads of house are, with the people who are picking up their particular things. But I respected him, and especially the breadth of his knowledge and experience." Ibis paused. "He was always very fair, which seems a pale compliment, but it meant a lot at the time." He flicked a finger against the table. "You?"

Pross would need to be as honest, she felt. She found his sudden openness startling, but it demanded a response in kind. She leaned forward, noticing her hand was quite close to his, on the small table, and having to restrain herself from reaching to touch him.

"I was the model of a very conventional Owl, really. Nose in my books, not much trouble for my teachers. Unusual in that I didn't really find a specialty, but it turns out that didn't matter. A good bookseller is often a generalist, interested in a bit of just about everything."

"A good researcher, too. You never know when something will come in handy."

Their order came. It was only after they'd divvied up the scones and Pross had taken a bit of time to inhale the spices of the chai and mix in the rich cream, that she spoke again. "So. Why are we here?"

Ibis let out a breath. "I am convinced that something is

up, at the Society. Something that is ... not correct." He frowned. "That's not quite the right word. Something is subtly wrong there. I can't pin down what it is."

"And why is that your concern?" Pross leaned forward. "I mean. You're a fellow."

"Because it, the things that are wrong there, once I had the conversation that made me question everything, they're... pervasive. Insidious. And the Society deserves better. Our community deserves better."

Pross frowned. "I'm not following, I think."

"I have, I admit, provided distractions. And not enough information for you to judge for yourself."

Pross murmured, "Some of those distractions were me." She gestured at the table. "So, lay out your points?"

Ibis beamed at her. "Those were very pleasant distractions. Oh, goodness, I hadn't said that, had I, I'd only thought it. Rather, I've been thinking it since we parted. I very much enjoy your particular sorts of distractions, but we should save that discussion for later. After we've talked to Master Hase."

Pross blinked several times. "You are an utterly ridiculous man, how am I supposed to concentrate now?" She was not at all sure she'd manage to, after frustratingly unspecific but clear sign of his interest.

"You, dear lady, are an Owl of the first water."

That made her laugh, and she replied, "Go on, your points. Give me something else to think about for the moment."

"What did you expect when you made the appointment at the Society? Every bit of it, based on what your husband told you, from writing to the meeting."

Pross considered. "I expected there to be a process, a structure. The Research Society exists to share scholarly resources, but also to help people with research questions that go beyond their own expertise. I assumed I would write, make an appointment, and meet with a scholar with suitable skills. Or perhaps the first meeting might be with an assistant or something of the kind, who could ask me more specific questions, and make those arrangements."

"And that's not what you got. What else did you expect? The space, the people..." He was clearly leading somewhere.

Pross chewed on her lip. "It was a lot more sparse than I expected. The waiting room, I know the Society has a significant collection of items. And books. And none of them were down there. I wouldn't expect delicate items, but there was nothing. No, you know, midrange art or wall hangings."

Ibis snorted. "They're all in Aimtree's room. And Lord Sisley, and his other favourites, I'm sure."

"Ibis?" Pross was baffled about different things now, at least, than her feelings.

"Lord Sisley's room has dozens of priceless artefacts and items in it. Aimtree has a number. It's Aimtree we're here about, specifically, but I'll wait to tell that part until we're talking to Master Hase."

"What about the process?" Pross wanted to come back to that.

"That too. You should have had an appointment with someone else, there's a rota. And they would have assigned you to someone. Each of us is supposed to take a certain number of consulting requests. And yet, very few people get as far as the initial appointment. Or a second."

"I did."

"But you had an idea how the Society was supposed to work, even if it was from a while ago. And I suppose they couldn't be sure if you were in contact with other people who'd been fellows when your husband was."

"Are you saying there's something wrong at the Society? Badly wrong?" He'd said that, but she needed to hear him admit it flat out.

Ibis looked up to meet her eyes, and then he nodded. "I am. I do think there is. I just don't know what. That's why we're here."

TWENTY-THREE

SCHOLA

Pross was nervous when they reached Master Hase's cottage. Ibis seemed oddly confident, leading her down the road, away from the village, and then knocking on the door. They'd spent the rest of their time talking through a timeline of their notes and experiences, but Ibis refused to explain what had them here now.

Master Hase could well be described as gangly and tall with long limbs and a sense of twitching attention. It was as if he was taking everything in. It was not dissimilar to the eternal vigilance she'd seen in people who'd served in the trenches in the War, or other places where danger could come at you from any direction. But Hase was too old to have served in that War.

He had shown them in, got them settled with sandwiches and more mugs of tea in comfortable chairs next to each other. It was as if this was something he did regularly, welcoming an old student and a stranger to talk about some topic or another. "A pleasure to have you here again so soon. And you must be Mrs Gates."

"Do we need to be formal? I'm Pross. Proserpina if you prefer a full name."

"Please, sir, do call me Ibis if you'd prefer."

Master Hase looked from one to the other. "I am Richart, then, if you can bring yourself to be informal, Ibis. In private, mind. We can't be giving the students ideas."

Ibis nodded, and then said, "Your note, sir, said you'd been able to observe the person I mentioned."

"I had. And you wrote this week, saying you'd had another encounter."

Pross looked from one to the other, baffled.

Ibis explained "This is about Aimtree, the one I'd mentioned before. This time, there were strange sensations, I asked Ma... Richart about them."

Pross must have looked very dubious, because Richart tilted his head, and said, "Here, Ibis, a question for you. How do you experience magic, then?"

Ibis shrugged, settling into what was clearly an old habit of conversation. "There isn't a good word in English, sir. A flicker of movement, a shimmer, around someone, when they're standing still, sometimes. A smell, sometimes, like after a thunderstorm. When it's stronger or very close, a sound like..." He paused. "That thing violins do, with the bow light on the strings."

Pross offered "Tremolo?" and he nodded.

"Some people see a shimmering light, or trails of magic, like streams." Master Hase settled back in his chair. "Do you get that around me? Around Pross?"

Ibis looked from one to the other, then tilted his head, considering, his eyes narrowing. "All around you, sir. But only her necklace, and her ring strongly. Otherwise a background sense. It has a sort of pulsing to the sound for you."

"Pross, dear lady?"

She blinked and said, "Me?"

"What do you sense? How do you sense it?"

"I get the light, sir, or a sense of gravity, of a slight pull, sometimes." She considered. "Mistress Howell, she trained me to follow my instinct, that that was magic, but it does not come with that kind of sensation."

"Oh, the pull, that's very interesting, I should suggest some reading to you. And what do you sense?"

"About the same, sir, for both of you. A shimmer of light. The light tells me different things, sometimes." Then she said, amused. "I wouldn't venture here. It's distracting."

"Anything different between us? Or between us and what you perceive with others?"

She frowned at that, and then said, uncertainly. "Not between you?" The tone in her voice made Ibis shift to take her hand in his. It was the first time he'd touched her like that, beyond the courtesies, and it startled her that he'd done what she hadn't dared. She glanced down at their hands before forcing herself to pay attention to Richart again. How had he been the one to do that?

That got a laugh, and a "Well. I suspect that the difference Ward here perceives but can't name is that I can do this."

He paused, took a breath. There was something Pross couldn't make her eyes focus on. There was a tiny popping sound and then the sudden appearance of a large hare. She squeezed Ibis's hand hard, painfully so. The hare blinked at them for a moment, leapt off the chair, bounded around the cottage several times, and then leapt again, transforming smoothly back into the man.

"Ward and I can do that." he said, cheerfully to Pross as he took his chair again. "And you can not."

Pross looked at Ibis, suddenly drawing her hand back,

and Ibis looked immediately ashamed. Fearful, even.
"Pross, I -"

She had to take a breath, then another, and Richart
murmured. "If you need a moment, fresh air or ..."

Pross nodded, pushing herself upright, then to the door
of the cottage, leaving it open behind her. She fumbled to
find the little bench beside the door, looking out to the
coastline. She had felt Ibis try to stand to follow her, and
heard just one comment from Richart, a "Patience."

Her head was swimming. It seemed a huge thing not to
know about someone. And yet he didn't owe her that, he
didn't owe her anything in particular.

Sitting there, looking off into the twilight, she felt in
over her head, fallen into a world that no longer made sense
in any possible dimension. She'd put so much into this, and
she'd thought she'd known what she was doing. It was so
clear in the last ten minutes that she hadn't understood
almost any of it.

It was several minutes before she felt ready to return.
When she came back, they were both sitting there,
completely quiet, though she could see they'd both drunk
half the tea in their cups. She closed the door behind her
and returned to her seat, smoothing her skirt down before
she said, "You have good reasons for not telling me, then?"

Ibis flinched at that, but said, "Yes, I do. You can guess
at many of them."

She waited, and clearly Richart would not try to inter-
vene, because the silence continued until Ibis spoke again.

"Seal House is associated with shape-shifting, but I
didn't learn at school. Only later, back in Egypt. It's, Master
Hase, Richart, can explain better, but people have affinities
for certain animals. I'm rather - honestly, I'm rather embar-
rassed by mine."

Pross raised an eyebrow, questioning.

Ibis took a deep breath, there was that same difficulty focusing on him, and then, sitting on the chair was a hedgehog. Bigger than the average, perhaps, a pale sandy colour. Pross almost reached out, but that seemed an intimacy she could not indulge in. Then she caught Richart gesturing with one hand, to show that she might reach out and let Ibis choose the interaction.

Pross half-knelt, to bring herself down to the level of the chair, and stretched out her hand. She left her hand resting on the chair, within reach. She could feel Ibis lean into her for a moment, before doing a little circle around the seat cushion, and shimmering again. When he was shaped like a man again, he took a breath, reaching to brush his hair out of his eyes.

"I see you've read a certain book, Ibis." Richart's voice was amused, even.

"Sir, yes, the man who taught me provided a copy."

Pross looked from one to the other, and Ibis broke into an explanation quickly enough that she wondered immediately what she must look like.

"There's a book, mentioned in Seal House, but otherwise quite obscure, that explains how to bring your clothes with you when you change forms. More precisely anything touching your skin, so anything you're holding. Otherwise, it is exceedingly embarrassing when you turn back."

"That would be like Bisclavet, then? Some other mediaeval werewolf myths? Though I suppose that's curses." The history was reassuring.

"Curses are different, yes." Ibis was amused for a moment before he returned to being a bit anxious. "You're not... upset?"

Pross considered. "Startled." she said, after a long pause.

"It's a rather large piece of information. But I've always rather thought hedgehogs a sensible sort of animal."

Ibis blinked at her.

"I suppose you'd rather turn into something dignified?"

"I had hopes of, well, an ibis. Or a raven if it had to be something British." She heard immediately that he was trying to be casual, to pass it off as something that didn't matter, and how much it did.

Pross couldn't help but laugh and laugh, and the way Ibis looked at her made her keep going until her side ached. When she caught her breath, she got out, "Ibis, by all the books, of course you turn into a hedgehog, have you met you? I've never seen anyone more suited."

Ibis looked at her wide-eyed, and there was utter silence for about ten seconds before he chortled. It began quietly, and then he was reaching for her hands, and laughing. It was such an honest and open sound, like layers of stone breaking away and letting something free.

When they both recovered their composure, Richart handed them each a cup of fresh tea. "Goodness." he said, dryly. "I do see why Ibis has spoken so well of you, Pross. There are not so many who will speak both kindly and bluntly to him."

Ibis looked at his old teacher, and then back at Pross. Pross felt suddenly pinned in place, by a different set of questions than the ones she'd been thinking about. There was something in being weighed by this man, and how he did it so naturally, that she found both terrifying and reassuring. It left her with some confidence she would not be left alone to sort this all out.

She ducked her chin and then tried to offer a beginning of something to Ibis. "We'll have to talk about some of it more later. I assume you don't tell people because it's a useful skill if people don't know about it."

Ibis nodded. "And hedgehogs are ... rather vulnerable," he said, more quietly. "Despite the spines."

Pross had a sudden flash of him telling her about being threatened. "That's why you were scared of the dog. Did you... after they attacked you, did you shift?"

Ibis was utterly startled, completely flatfooted, but then he nodded, looking away. "Yes."

Pross reached out a hand to touch his cheek, venturing the intimacy, even with Richart watching.

"Well, then. Had it occurred to you that a hedgehog would also fit rather well into, say, a woman's handbag?"

By the look he gave her, he clearly hadn't.

TWENTY-FOUR

SCHOLA

"So, why is the shape-shifting relevant now?" Pross was clearly not going to let herself be too distracted. Ibis watched the way her eyes narrowed, the little lines in her forehead as she frowned in concentration.

Ibis glanced at Richart, then said, "I believe my esteemed teacher was trying to lead me towards recognising that Aimtree is also a shifter."

"People who shift can generally learn to spot others who can. Those who use the same method of shifting, and often other methods, such as the selkies, or werefolk, or shape-shifting curses."

Pross said, her tone a little wobbly, "I feel like I've fallen into an entirely new world. I'd always heard that ..." Her voice trailed off. Ibis hesitated for a second, but he wanted, needed, to offer more reassurance, and reached out a hand to cover hers. He could feel her turn her hand to take his as Richart replied.

"Most people think shape-shifting a myth, or the sort of legendary magic that is no longer at all common. It's more common than that, but for many reasons people don't talk about it."

Ibis murmured, "There are insults. that people who can shift are - less human. Less in general. Somehow more of an animal."

He wasn't sure what to make of the fact that Pross immediately said, "They did that to you. I mean, already. You didn't need to give them more reasons."

Richart tapped his fingers on the arm of the chair, visibly deciding. "I will tell you something rarely shared outside the Heads of House here. Each House has its own magics and secrets, you know that much, and things that they specialise in."

Pross looked up, hesitantly. "Sir?"

"One requirement to become head of Seal House is the ability to see who can shape-shift. In practice, that means that the head usually is a skilled shifter themselves, though there have been exceptions here and there over the centuries."

"Huh." That was clearly a puzzle Pross would chew on for weeks, but it gave Ibis a chance to redirect the conversation. "So, sir, Richart, you've been leading toward the suggestion that Aimtree can also shift."

"It seems very likely. Something reptile, you mentioned scales."

"Do you think he knows I can?" Ibis did not like that thought at all. Pross reached out to take his hand and squeeze it.

"Aimtree was not in our house, so I do not know how he learned. On the whole, those who learn outside our house have fewer of the ... oh, one might reasonably call the auxiliary skills. Sensing other shifters, keeping belongings handy, being able to shift while walking or moving, or being able to control details of our animal shape."

"Details?" He was not at all surprised that Pross found this curious, that she wanted to learn more. And he loved, again, how she asked for what she needed. She was leaning forward now, glancing between Richart and Ibis.

"The general theory." He paused, clearly amused. "We have not time for a proper discussion about it tonight. I can lend you some books. The theory is that people have an affinity for certain kinds of animals. Those who polish certain skills may control the colour of the animal or markings. Highly skilled shifters who learn young can take on perhaps half a dozen forms, but most people have one or two at most. And usually one of those is much preferred above the others." Richart had slipped easily into lecture mode.

"Can you give me an example?"

"Oh, I know a number of people who turn into a small cat and a larger cat, for example. Often to blame for tales among non-magical folk of panthers stalking the moors."

Pross laughed at that. "Oh, I suppose."

Ibis coughed. "We do have a more immediate problem?"

Richart nodded. "Two questions, then. First, did you get the same sense about Sisley? And second, tell me what you saw in their offices."

That took Ibis aback. "No, as to Sisley. Something seemed... off about him, but not the same way as Aimtree. Like..." Ibis considered. "The wrong temple incense, sir," he said finally. "I don't know how to put it better than that. It wasn't a smell, exactly."

"Trust your instincts there, they're serving you well. Does Aimtree have anything similar?"

"Aimtree wears an overwhelming cologne." Ibis's voice

was very dry.

"Ah, well. The rooms?"

Ibis frowned. "They weren't what I expected. They were both stuffed with items, notable items, from the Society collections. That was not the case in the past, those things used to be in the public spaces and on display, Pross believes."

Richart nods. "What is it like now?"

"A lot of bare walls." Pross's voice was flat. "Everywhere, not just some places. And Ibis has an office up in what used to be servants quarters, under the roof, and I gather most of the other rooms get little use."

Ibis glanced at her and said, "I'm used to it."

"It's still insulting." She would be stubborn about it, from the set of her jaw and how she tucked one arm against her waist. She was so fierce when she thought someone had given offence, even the slights he'd learned long ago weren't worth arguing over.

"The offices?" Richart's voice was quiet, but he was determined about this.

"It was not what I expected. There were a wider range of cultures than I expected. Not Egyptian, not Nubian, but..." He frowned, thinking back. "Mesopotamian. I'd have to look at books more, to figure out whether it was Babylonian or Assyrian or Sumerian."

"Any particular iconography?"

"There was one panel." Ibis said after a long moment. "The sirrush - I'm afraid I can't manage the other name as easily. Associated with Marduk. I could sketch it."

Richart shook his head. "No, I think I know the one." He stood up, going to the bookshelves and coming back with an archaeological journal, flipping through the pages, and then opening to a black and white sketch.

"Like that, yes. The background tiles were a rich blue, and the sirrush was a coppery beige, and there were some red tiles around the edges."

"Curious." Richart was non-committal beyond that.

Pross settled back in her chair, frowning. Ibis leaned forward. "Are you all right?"

"You said Mesopotamian."

"I did."

"That seems very..." She frowned. "That sort, at least as you've described them, are generally very British. The Empire as the pinnacle of civilisation. Oh, they'll nod to Rome and to Greece, as the stones we built on, and certainly aqueducts and hot water were grand, but nothing like what we have now. What do they specialise in?"

Ibis shook his head. "Aimtree's doing a catalogue of Georgian shoe buckles," he said. "Lord Sisley...." He shook his head. "He's done a variety of things in the past, if I remember right."

Richart coughed, and said "I have some useful information, here."

"Sir?" Ibis couldn't repress the title.

"We do keep records. When you mentioned Sisley, I had a look." He made a considering face again. "You are, neither of you, inclined to tell people gossip who shouldn't hear it. You both keep your tongues."

"Sir." This came out at the same time as Pross's "Of course."

"We've been, well, dubious, shall we say, of Sisley's research record for some time now. He's turned out a variety of pieces, every couple of years, and often changing fields. Never so dramatically to make one certain, but enough to make one wonder if it's one of the old nasty stories in research."

Pross saw it more quickly. "He's taking other people's work."

"Yes. Do you know who the fellows were before you, Ibis?"

Ibis frowned. "A few names. One of them left in some disgrace, some sort of breakdown, but no one has told me the details. They do not confide in me."

"I suspect they hoped to use your work, and you're too canny for that. And too habituated to locking your door and keeping personal possessions on you."

Pross settled into thinking about something, Ibis realised, as he glanced over. She was frowning, concentrating, then reached into her bag and drew out her notebook, flipping through as if looking for something she hadn't seen the point in indexing earlier. While she did, he replied, "Habit, as you say. And a healthy one, it sounds like. Do you believe they're a direct threat?"

"Possibly. It would do no harm to take suitable precautions. Or rather, continue to take precautions." Richart nodded at Pross. "I'm sure the lady does, I know you do."

"Sir?"

"That would be telling." It was gently said, teasing, in a way Ibis hadn't heard in a long time, like his father had. "I have my own connections, you realise."

"I wouldn't expect anything else, sir." Ibis glanced at Pross. "While she's thinking, sir, I had a question about the shifting."

Richart laughed and they turned to nuances of a few texts for a good twenty minutes, before Pross coughed and said, "Pardon, I think I've found it."

Ibis looked up, and stopped talking in the middle of a sentence, so he could immediately hear what she'd come up with.

Richart nodded at her. "Go ahead. More tea?"

She nodded absently, and then said, "Ibis, you remember that reference that Lizzie tracked down for me? The barbarian?"

Ibis blinked. "Yes? The one that clearly referenced the source of an item, something not Roman, but also not British."

Pross nodded. "The citations Lizzie found for me, they clarify that it would indicate something not-Greek and not-Roman. What if that's something... something from another ancient culture?"

"Mesopotamia?"

Pross shrugged. "Perhaps. And I found the description. A tube, made of some sort of stone. There's a reference to jacinte - I'd have to do more reading, but I think it means darker than that. Darker blue? Lapis Lazuli or azurite or some such?"

Richart raised an eyebrow.

"One has to know one's pigments if you deal with older books." Her tone was a little prim, before she added, with a smile. "Also, I thought that was a fun part. Learning to powder the stones and make paint."

"So." Ibis was working to keep up. "We have some indications they have interests in something Mesopotamian. There may be such an item in the hoard. Which explains why they want to keep people away. But they... why haven't they dug it up?" The way her mind worked, how she pieced things together, that was glorious, when she trusted herself. His was a plodding sort of research, meticulous and detailed, and her mind made the pictures live.

Pross snorted. "They don't know where it is. And not actually being competent researchers, never mind archaeologists, they can't find it without our help."

TWENTY-FIVE

LONDON

The discussion had gone on well into the evening, and it was nearly ten when they found themselves on the doorstep again.

Pross turned to Ibis. "What do we do - I mean, we still have things to talk about?"

He nodded. "I was thinking." His voice turned careful and shy. "Would you come back to my flat? We can get there by portal and a short walk."

"Which we can't to my home. Is that, are you sure?"

It certainly seemed like he was making at least something of a proposition. Privacy and discretion. She knew there were reasons not to do this. But she only had to look at him, in the flickering light of the charm lantern on the road, to want to go with him. And besides, they did have a lot to talk about.

"My flatmate's doing a long shift at the hospital. He won't be home until tomorrow afternoon. We'll be quite private. I'll take the couch, of course, or there's a little inn with rooms around the corner." It was clear Ibis was doing his best to persuade. She realised with a start that it was the first time he'd asked her for something personal.

Pross pursed her lips, then let herself smile. "I packed a change of clothes. I can never tell what will come up when I'm with you."

He was watching her, so intently. "Does that mean...." His voice trailed off.

She snorted and reached for his hand. "That means I was expecting to need to be spontaneous. Come on. Your flat it is."

The next twenty minutes were a rush, both of them walking back to the portal. Ibis told the portal keeper the address, the portal near the Royal Society.

"This way." His idea of a short walk was about what she expected, leading her up half a mile, past the university and into the realm of the hospital. She could hear people around them, the noises of the city settling down for the night. He ducked into an old alleyway, something that must have predated the Great Fire, and up into the second floor of a Georgian house.

The flat itself was much as she expected, once she got a look at it, and rather like his office but with better furniture. It wasn't fancy, but the couch was clearly not a bad bed in a pinch. The colours of the room were muted blues and greens and browns, a deliberate choice. There were two desks with books and tall bookshelves. All in all, things were quite tidy. She glanced around, but saw only one household shrine. By the statues, it was clear it belonged to Ibis. "That's Hathor, isn't it?"

He blinked at her, and then again, like he wasn't quite sure she was real, suddenly. "Hetheru." he agreed. "Goddess of many things, but including beauty."

She considered, for just a moment, and then ventured a leap. "Also of love." There was no way to ask that didn't sound arch. "Will you, with me?"

"Before we talk?"

"Some things do not need words." Pross felt everything go crystal clear. She wanted this man, now, in this place. She wanted to throw herself into something gloriously impulsive with him. She had been patient, and well-behaved and doing all the things she was told, for so long. This, now, they were grown adults, they suited so well.

He loosened his jacket, then shrugged it off, tossing it over the end of the couch, holding his hands out to her. "I'm willing. More than willing. If you wish."

She could see in that moment that he still thought she would turn away. Instead, she took the two steps toward him, took his hand, lacing her fingers through his. She slid the other around his back, standing on tip toe, wanting to kiss him again.

He made her reach for it for just long enough to worry her, before he steered her, as if he were in some intricate dance he was unfurling for her. She found herself with her back to the wall by the door, and then he was bending, to kiss, pressing against her, enticing her. His hand slipped down to cup her hip, then dipped to lift her skirt. "All of it? All of you?"

"All." She breathed it out in his ear. "It's safe, with you."

"Oh, very," he said. He rolled his hips against her, and she could feel, intimately and intensely that he was drawing this out, but not because he did not want.

"How?"

There was a slow drawl in his voice, something utterly contented. "I had a dream of pressing you against this wall, and then taking you to my bed, sprawling out with you. Seeing - will you ride me, will you stretch out and let me delight you? You are not predictable, you know." His voice was rough as he came to the end, and he bent to kiss her again, more urgently, leaning into her, with a pressure of body and desire.

She arched against the wall, and suddenly her clothing was too much. Some small distant part of her mind thought this was madness, but if it was, it felt divine. There was nothing she wanted more than to see where this took them. Together.

"A dream?" Her voice turned purring. "Let us see about the real thing."

His hand slipped between them, reaching to undo her dress, deft enough with it that he'd clearly had more than a little experience undoing a woman's clothes. She inhaled sharply, then murmured, "What should I know, your past?"

Ibis laughed. "I was as diligent at learning pleasure as learning archaeology."

She could see that same wild joy from earlier that afternoon in him, something free and utterly at ease, and she wanted more of it. "It's been... well. Since my husband."

"I won't rush you, then. Too much." She shifted to look at him better, and his eyes were dancing, before he moved to let her up from the wall. "My bedroom is there." He gestured with his chin.

"Show me?" Her heart was racing, now, the way they were with each other, both sharp and attentive, and observant. The way he honed her, made her keep on her toes, to follow where he led, that delighted her, and aroused her. She could feel her breasts swelling against her bandeau, and how her breath was catching.

He took her hand, drawing her with him, down the hall

and into a room with a tall window. It too was in the muted
shades he clearly favoured, river and tree and sandy brown.
The bed would be narrow for two people, but they would
make it work. He closed the door, murmuring "Lavatory is
the first door on the left."

"Considerate," she murmured, and ventured to nibble
at his ear when he bent to undo the button of his trousers.

He moaned, startling them both, before his hands
worked at her clothes instead. Piece by piece, they unfas-
tened each other, leaving an untidy pile by the end of the
bed. Her dress and underthings, his trousers and shirt. He
turned for a moment to drop cufflinks into a tiny box on his
dresser, then back to her. His face was lit up, entirely
focused on her, taking her in. It should make her blush, it
should embarrass her, and yet it didn't, it made her want to
arch and preen and display herself for him.

"By all the names, you're gorgeous." He breathed it out.

"You, I've.... in Paris, you looked so ..." She ran out of
words, and before she could try again, he bent to kiss her.
He pressed her back against the bed so she was perching on
it, and then lying back, diagonally along it, with his body
between her legs.

He had a plan, she could tell immediately, because he
settled along her. He traced the curve of her breast, stopping before her nipple, watching her expression intently,
studying every reaction. "What do you like, then?" he
asked. "Or shall we uncover it together?"

The tone in his voice, how contented it was, full and
focused on her. It made her shiver, and then, to her dismay,
she could feel tears at the corners of her eyes.

Ibis noticed immediately. "Too much?" His hand
paused, he didn't draw back, but he didn't press on.

She took a moment to form words, to remember how to

speak. "Not enough. Please. More now. Talking later. Please." Her voice broke on the last word, it came out entirely as begging.

"Let me touch you, then." His voice had got quiet.

She opened her eyes, searching his face. Had she made him angry? No, that intensity was still there, but it was focused now. His movements were different, less light touch, more pressure, that she found easier to open to.

Ibis let his left hand drifted down to her abdomen, then her hip, while he kissed steadily down from her shoulder around the curve of her breast. His thumb brushed along one of the stretch marks, and he lifted his head, then smiled, murmuring, "You have history in your skin," Like it was a glorious new thing to learn.

At that, she could only give herself over to what they were doing, arching her neck for his kisses. As his lips moved, as they closed around her nipple, she cried out, the sensation utterly different than before. This was not her child or her child's father, this was so intimate, and yet new and splendid for it to be him. She drew her arm around his shoulders, letting her fingers trace patterns on his back.

"Oh, yes, please." Ibis was murmuring, over and over again, encouraging her. She could feel his cock between them, against her side. There was a spreading spot of his fluids and his fingers were dipping to tease her. Then one was pressing inside her and it made her moan.

She wasn't sure how long it was before he drew back and murmured. "May I stand? So I, so I can touch? Is that..." His voice trailed off, and she saw what he wanted, how they were angled.

Pross drew one knee up to her chest, letting him press between her legs, then settled her leg around his hip. "Let's try." She was more than willing to see what he had in mind.

The position let him press into her, steady and even, and it was glorious. Before he was halfway in, she was caught up in the sensation, the fullness. She could feel herself clenching around him, heard herself cry out sharply, and the rush of her climax overwhelmed her.

Ibis thought there was nothing more beautiful in the world than her expression, how she was giving herself over to pleasure. He thought of one of the many prayers to Hetheru he'd learned over the years, a line beating in his head. *I was joyful, exulting, elated, when they said "See, She is here."*

It took all his self control not to climax in that moment, a rush of sensation sweeping over him, like a brush of stars against skin. He focused on her, on watching how her face changed and opened. The smile on her face amazed him when she relaxed in the aftermath, and opened her eyes again, focusing on him. Only then did he pull back, and begin to rock in and draw out, settling into a gentle rhythm.

"Ibis..." Her voice was breathy, and he reached down to brush his fingers against her cheek. That's why he'd wanted them like this, so he could reach and touch her, not need to hold himself up on his arms.

"Lady." It was both to the lady in his bed, and the one he'd honoured since he was a child.

"This, oh, yes." She had been attempting to say something, but how they were moving together, that was a different joy.

"More, then?" He couldn't help laughing, feeling the joy still rolling through him, like he was filling up with light and magic. Perhaps he was.

She arched her hips, and he took the hint, picking up his pace and doing his best to press deeper. He felt her legs tighten around him, how she didn't want to let him go.

"Oh, oh, yes." She was building up again, beautifully responsive now she allowed herself to be.

It was only then he shifted, reaching to touch her breast with one hand, tease at it, the other shifting to stroke her skin, to touch and inflame her more. "More, then?" he asked again.

This time she snorted and tightened her legs. "More and more and more. Oh, please, more." Her voice was earthy, now, not demanding, but offering and sharing.

Beautiful as she was to him, he found that even more stunning, how she gave herself once she chose, and how fully. He bent down, sucking at her other nipple now, testing her reactions, and bucking once as her fingers tightened in his hair. She wasn't shy of being as active as she could be, touching him as freely as he touched her.

Part of him wished he could do this forever, and yet, he wanted to build and drive and seek new heights of pleasure. Once he felt her responding to him, quivering in his arms, he murmured "More."

Only then did he pull back to plant his feet, use his hands to reposition her, put her hips just where he hoped, and begin to thrust.

Her eyes opened again, and now she was watching him, intently. All of her doing her best to move with him once she got the sense of his pace, letting the movements rock her body. Soon, her sighs and whimpers were perfect punctuation.

He'd hoped, he'd wanted her to be like this, to be as direct and clear in bed as she was out of it. If anything, she was more so, eager and needy again as he built up toward his climax. Finally, he let the need and want and desire and raw lust overwhelm him. He let his hips thrust and pump, then let himself crest, bucking into her several times, utterly at the mercy of his desires.

His knees went weak, and he barely managed to rotate them both. He used the last of his strength to press into her and hold as the final shudders of his body finished. They were stretched out on the bed, as he slipped his hand between them to stroke her, finding the right touch in the last moments of his ability to think. He felt her contract around him, shiver against him, as he let himself fall to her side, pulling her tighter to him and letting his eyes close.

He could hear the sound of the earliest morning outside when he half-woke to find her shifting position, stretching out so one hand draped off the edge of the bed. "Mmmm." It was a contented sound. "No couch?"

"No couch." It made him laugh, the absurdity of it all, then he asked, "May I kiss you?"

"Again." Now she was laughing, until he felt for her and found her shoulder, then brushed his fingers against her cheek, then lips. He took his time with it, lingering, enjoying the mysteries of the darkness with her.

When he pulled back, he murmured, "Was that good? Being spontaneous?"

"Oh, very. Grand encouragement to do it some more." Her voice was throaty and warm. "Surely, you don't doubt your skills here?"

He shrugged, not that she could see it, and then couldn't think of anything to say.

She reached for him, squeezing his hand once she found it. "It was wonderful. Again, sometime. That, and much more."

He inhaled, sharply, because this was the talking they needed to do, and he wasn't sure it was the right time, and yet. "What does this mean to you?"

Pross let out a long sigh, wriggling against him to stretch out better. "I was thinking, as I woke up, about all the places we could go together. Once Cammie's in school."

"Places?"

"Would you show me Egypt? Or is that too much? There's Hungary. Vienna. More Paris, there's a lot of Paris we haven't seen together yet. And I've never been to so many other places. There are whole other continents."

This was not what Ibis had expected, exactly. "Travelling?"

"I already know you're wonderful to travel with. You notice things, you enjoy good food, and the really interesting things, not just the currently fashionable. I kept - you know, I kept thinking back to walking down the Seine with you, and talking about how the city grew."

Ibis blinked at her, in the dark, so it did him little good. "That's what convinced you?"

"The sex is also exceedingly good, the research skills exemplary, and you are an adorable hedgehog." Her tone was deadpan. Just as she finished, she summoned a light into her hand. From the way she peered up at him, it was so she could watch his expression. He suspected he looked even more flatfooted than he felt.

She set the light to hover by the bed and shifted to her

side so she could reach him better. "It doesn't bother you?" Ibis asked, checking.

She settled her hand in his. "Is it supposed to?"

"You were upset, when I told you." Ibis felt that this was an important part of the data, and impossible to ignore.

"I was." Pross went quiet, letting her thumb trace along his hand while she rummaged for words. "It was a surprise. A big one. Both the fact that's not just a legend, and the fact you do it."

He almost said something, but she shook her head. "I was upset, and then I had to go think about it, to figure out what I was feeling, and why I was upset, and what to do about it that made sense."

He hesitated, but he had to ask. "What made it all right?"

"That you were honest with me then. You let me see. You were... " She paused. "I know I don't understand some of this. But you chose to be vulnerable, to let me see a thing you've kept hidden so carefully. You trusted me with that."

"My family knows. But that's it." he said. He hadn't talked about this with anyone but them for so long. "In the War, people who shifted were..." He had to stop. "A lot of them died. Horribly, the ones we know about."

Pross inhaled sharply, she clearly hadn't even thought about that aspect. "Oh."

"I used it. I just... told no one. And I think the people who could shift, they didn't tell on others." He gestured. "The Schola memorial plaque. It's evenly split between the houses. If people had told about all the shifters, it wouldn't be."

She flinched at that. "More Boar and Bear than the others, but ... that's what you'd expect, by reputation." she agreed. "Charging into danger, if for different reasons."

Ibis nodded. "So I went into Intelligence. My language skills, they were very useful in Egypt. But I suspect they'd have thought those - replaceable, if they'd known about the other."

Pross rolled a little, to hug him tightly, burrowing against his shoulder. "Glad you had the choice."

He stroked down her back. "So. Besides the travel." He heard her let out her breath, take another.

"We have some practical challenges." Pross was cautious. "But I - I look forward to time with you. More than I wanted to admit. I don't know what it looks like though."

"We do have some things to solve. But I could come out there most weekends. Or longer depending on if they pull the fellowship. If you wanted."

She blinked at him, trying to make things sort out in her head.

"I enjoy my fellowship, I'm doing useful research, I wouldn't have access to the Petrie collection without it. But there are other things I can do, and I'm not ... dependent on the stipend. Naturally frugal, more than anything."

"Except for the little pleasures that breathe," she pointed out.

He beamed at her and rewarded that with a kiss. "Good beer. Very important, beer. Do you want one?"

"It's ... four in the morning? No." But she was laughing now, the tension gone. "So. What would you do with yourself instead?"

"I stayed in England so Hypatia would have family near enough, for holidays and, well, helping arrange an apprenticeship contract. But I can do that in the Trellech clubs if I have to. I've enough connections now, I think."

Pross considered that, and then she said, "What will she think of this?"

"She'll tell me she was right all along. She swore I was interested in you - well, you remember when I went out in February?"

Pross laughed. "Goodness."

"And your daughter?"

"That is more complicated. I'm honestly not sure." She shook her head, and Ibis lent to kiss her again.

"We can sort that out later. Talk it through together. Now, you should get some more sleep."

Pross heard the door open. It was much later that morning, nearly eleven, and Ibis had left her in the kitchen to cut up some ham and mushrooms and cheese for omelettes.

"Ibis, love?"

The head that appeared around the corner of the kitchen was not Ibis, but rather a tall black man, wearing a jacket and shirt and trousers.

She stepped back. "Um?"

"You must be Mrs Gates? I'm Jonas." The man was all amiability, now. Also, once he spoke, very American.

"You..." She tried to gather her thoughts. "You must be Ibis's flatmate? He said you weren't off duty until three?" Then she remembered her manners. "Yes, I'm - do call me Pross, please? Short for Proserpina, which is a mouthful at the best of times." She knew she was babbling. "Ibis just went out to get bread, he discovered you were out."

"I took the last bit for sandwiches." Jonas was very amiable about it. Clearly it was something they did sometimes.

Pross let out a long breath. "So. Omelette? We've enough eggs for three?"

"That'd be great. Tea? I admit, I've got fond of the national obsession with the stuff."

Pross closed her eyes for a moment, then nodded. "The kettle's on, I don't know how long yours takes." She was trying for normality, and not quite succeeding.

It was then she heard the door again. "Pross, are you... Jonas!" Pross couldn't tell if it was pleasure or startlement. "Um. I asked Pross to stay. You weren't here, you said you'd be back at three."

"Tricky case came in, they called in the big guns, sent me away." Jonas waved a hand and shook his head.

"The usual annoyance, then." Ibis clearly had heard this before. "Pross, here's the bread, fresh out of the bakery. Oh, that looks grand."

They had a rhythm, the two of them. After a moment, Pross stepped out of the way, and let them go to work, cracking eggs, and adding onion, then cooking in the ham and cheese and mushrooms. Ibis murmured directions on the pot of tea, and she could at least set that up without feeling entirely in the way and out of place.

It wasn't until they were seated, awkwardly, three at a table designed for two, that Jonas said, "You weren't expecting me, I know."

Ibis spoke up. "We could use your good sense."

Jonas raised an eyebrow.

Pross tilted her head, and Ibis continued, "We were talking to the master of my house at school last night. And there is a ... method for Pross to allow me to listen in. Is that worth taking, do you think?"

Jonas looked Pross up and down, and it was a curious sort of gaze. She was used to men weighing her beauty, or her lack thereof, or her presentation. This was something different. "To go back out to the property?"

Ibis nodded. "We have an idea what they're looking for."

Jonas frowned, then popped the last of his omelette in his mouth to chew while he was thinking. "The right sort of clothes, the right sort of formality, it might work. I don't know the right idiom here. My aunts would wear a hat, and a little veil, and a tailored dress or maybe a suit. Is tweed the thing?" It had an inquiring lilt to it.

"Your aunts?"

"Pillars of a certain portion of Philadelphia society. Quite capable of walking into a bank or a store or something else and shaming people into decency just by standing there. When they speak, it's much more terrifying."

Pross shifted in her chair. "You're saying, turn up looking very professional, as much as I can, on an afternoon on muddy paths." She paused, then admitted. "Tweed is probably the thing. Well, tweed and a permission letter from my client."

"And you agree with whatever this method is Ibis had in mind?"

Pross couldn't help grinning foolishly at Ibis. "Oh, yes. I suggested it."

Jonas looked from one to the other, then said, "Couch? I want to sketch something."

"Sketch?"

"Ibis showed me some of the maps. I think I have an idea on the best route to take."

Pross moved over to the couch, and a moment later, Ibis settled next to her. He rested his hand on his leg in the kind of nonchalant position that allowed her to choose whether or not to touch him. She took the opportunity, fitting her hand against his.

Jonas brought a small table over, a large map, and several pieces of tracing paper, then made a copy of the walking maps. "You said you think the hoard is here, or here, or here." he said, making a small dot on each one. Ibis leaned over and nodded.

"And these, here, the blue lines, those are the public walking paths. This is the road. How close do you need to get?"

Ibis frowned. "To get a sense of the land." he said. "Both a view at a distance, and closer in."

"There's an elevation, here, from a public road." Jonas indicated it after peering at the ordnance map. "And these spots, they should let you get good views of the site. Where did they stop you, last time?"

Ibis leaned to peer at the map again. "There." he said, pointing with his free hand. "That walking path, about halfway between the two roads."

"Where did they come from?"

This was more of a mystery to Ibis, and Jonas frowned. "You are not used to thinking about the dangers in the woods and fields," he said, finally.

Ibis looked up sharply, "Pardon?"

Jonas waved his hand. "I think they must have come from here. There's a building marked on the map, a smaller house? Is this the manor?" Pross moved to look at the map, and she nodded.

"Does anyone live there?"

Pross shook her head. "There's a caretaker, in a cottage on the property - that one, there, I think. But I don't know if the caretaker's the person who ran Ibis off. Philly implied it was a woman, with a man for odd jobs as they came up."

Ibis murmured, "That's a new piece of information."

"I did do some work between Paris and Schola, ta." Pross was teasing, but she felt him stiffen, and she reached for his hand.

Jonas looked from one to the other and said, "Look, I was up all night. Thanks for the food, I'm going to go to bed. Ibis, let me know when you'll be out, and when I should worry, okay?"

Ibis nodded, rather absently, and Pross watched him well after Jonas had disappeared first into the bathroom, then into the bedroom at the other end of the hall.

"Sorry." Ibis almost pulled away, putting more distance between them.

"What are you sorry for?" Pross was confused now.

"Jonas. And we're still sorting ourselves out."

Pross let out a breath. "Oh, Ibis. Honestly." She felt rather that was being a trifle dense. "Jonas is lovely. We startled each other, but that happens, it's fine." There was something else wrong here, but she couldn't figure it out. She just knew, by watching the tension back in his jaw, and in his hands.

"I haven't told Jonas."

"I assumed not. That's why I didn't explain the details of the plan, just the - relevant requirements."

Ibis went still for a long moment, then said, "You meant it, that ... you don't mind?"

"I meant that I think you're adorable. Like that, just like you are now. Prickly, mind. But adorable."

That earned her a kiss on the cheek, a quick peck. "Adorable is not the word I'd have picked?"

"You lack a certain perspective on yourself. Everyone does."

Ibis frowned. "Still. Adorable." He didn't like that, that much was obvious.

"Not an adjective you're fond of?"

Ibis shook his head. "Nor a shape."

Pross considered. "Don't they have hedgehogs in Egypt? I could have sworn I'd seen something. When we went to the museum, even."

That earned her a very dubious look.

"It isn't an elegant bird - and you're right, a raven would have been fascinating, they're brilliant. But you are very much a hedgehog, love." It was the last word that helped more than the rest, she suspected.

"You're going to be stubborn about this being fine, aren't you?"

"Well, yes. Because it is. And you're going to be grumpy about it, because that's how you are."

Ibis snorted, in better humour. Being given her blessing for grumpiness helped. "What do we do next, then?"

"We figure out when we're going up to Norwich. Not today, I need to go home and excavate my closet. Oh, and get a letter from Philly, and probably get one of my walking shoes repaired, and find a suitably large bag."

"Next week? Longer?"

"Maybe next weekend, maybe longer. I suspect it will depend on Philly. Will you be all right at the Society?"

"I don't think they're going to bash me over the head and drag me down into the tunnels under the city and sacrifice me, no. But I expect the usual round of embarrassment and nasty remarks, and having to justify everything I do or don't do, or how I do it." He paused. "I'm more or less used to that."

"If we get this right, maybe more sensible people will

end up in charge." She paused. "Are there more sensible people, actually?"

Ibis frowned, thinking about that question. "There are people who aren't very active right now. I don't know much about them."

"Send me a list. If I don't know them, maybe Carillon does. He's very handy that way."

TWENTY-EIGHT

A TRAIN TO NORWICH

The following Saturday, they got a compartment together on the decidedly non-magical train from London to Norwich.

Ibis had hoped they might manage Friday night together, but Pross had written Thursday morning to say she had an appointment on Friday that would last until dark. Nothing more than that. He had worried about what it might mean, but he'd not had time to ask. She'd shown up ten minutes before the 8am train left, wearing a light tweed walking suit, in a striking forest green, looking entirely proper and not at all matronly.

Pross had with her a leather knapsack, rather than a handbag, and a walking stick. She wore a straw hat on her head that was more optimistic about the amount of sun they might get than Ibis was. It was not actively raining, but it looked as if it might.

It was only once they'd got through the fuss of having their tickets ready, and settling their things, that they could talk.

"Are you ..." "What do you..." collided, and Pross smiled, and said "You first."

Ibis swallowed, then said, "That's not a handbag." It came out more accusing than he meant it to.

"Better than a handbag." she said. "Look."

She passed the bag over to him, and he took it. It was lighter than it looked. That part was magical, surely, because it was quite full. There were a few metal tins. "Lunch?" he asked, looking up, and she nodded. Then she reached over and hooked a small width of cloth across the top of the bag. It looked almost like an added cover against the rain, but when she pushed her hand down on it, it made a hammock. Big enough, he realised, for a hedgehog.

"The flap doesn't come down tightly, so you should be able to see, if we're careful. If someone stops me, you can get into the lower area, see here? And there's a rivet here, it looks like it's supposed to be part of the fastening, but maybe you can look out."

Again, she was perhaps optimistic, but he looked at it more closely. "That's brilliant." It was. And thoughtful, he'd expected to be clinging onto whatever was provided, or perhaps be uncomfortably tucked in a pocket.

"How long can you...?" she asked, her voice trailing off.

"Stay like that? Oh, days, if I need to. But I need to eat things suitable to the form. And it takes a lot of energy to maintain it."

Pross considered, then said, "I brought a lot of sandwiches."

Despite being more nervous about this than he wanted to admit, that made him laugh. "It's about two hours to Norwich, so we should be there by ten. It's about an hour's walk to the first place Jonas marked."

"Let's sort out where we want to go in what order." She

reached into the bag, and drew out the maps, both the ordnance surveys and Jonas's path, then a watercolour journal for him to write on. She handed him a pencil.

He stared at it, unsure what she was thinking.

"You've been there before. And you're the archaeologist. Consider me your carriage."

"And protector against dogs."

The thought delighted her and she grinned. "If you'll permit, kind sir."

"You'll notice things too." He felt this was important to keep in mind.

"I hope so. But I don't know how to tell what's important." She paused, then added, "I brought a watercolour set with me. I'm not bad with a quick sketch, for how the land lies."

"Unexpected talents!" He was startled, though perhaps he shouldn't be. She'd shown a good eye for art in the books she'd selected.

It earned him a smile. "One skill of a well-brought up lady that's actually useful sometimes."

That made him laugh before they settled in to work. They spent a good forty minutes going through the maps, the sequence that made the most sense. "May I see your hand? Or rather, can you put your thumb here? And here? And here?" She looked baffled, but did as he asked.

Ibis made several notations on the maps, and said, "In each case, the spot I actually want to look at is the width of your thumb above the point marked. Will you remember that?"

She saw his point at once. "So that if they demand to see the maps or something, we're not pointing at anything specific."

"Exactly. I wasn't able to bring tools, or some of the

magical devices that assist archaeology. I don't own them myself, we'd have to figure out something for those, though there are some people who might lend me enough. But it will give us enough to know where to focus when we can do that."

Pross nodded. "I might have some connections, too."

"Your Lord Carillon?" Ibis was curious. He'd asked around about the man. "He's got a confusing reputation."

"Geoffrey has always delighted in having layers." It was the fondness of a sister. "What did you hear?"

"I mentioned to several people I'd been out to True Eyeworth, and had heard he was improving things in the area, so this is all in passing. Most of them were certain he's nothing more than a well-meaning aristocrat, a decent one for that kind. Pavo and horses and nice clothing. There was some scandal about his wife's family, but not her directly?"

"The Penhallow expedition that disappeared was her father and uncle. A lot of people lost money. You'll like her, when you can meet her. Well, Geoffrey too. What else?"

"I ran into someone who wouldn't tell me much, just that he was much sharper than expected. No details."

"I must tell his lordship he slipped up."

Ibis snorted, and they passed a few minutes looking out at the countryside.

Pross cleared her throat, and then said, rather hesitantly, "How much are you - you? When you're like that?" He noticed she wasn't coming out and saying the word 'shape-shifting' which was probably all to the good. Railway cars were not nearly as private as might be.

"My mind is mine, but ... thinking about how to do things is different, sometimes. The solutions I come up with."

Pross nodded. "How do you want to play getting to Norwich?"

"I don't think they'll be watching for me at the train station. Find somewhere out of the way, and I'll change, and you can follow the map?"

She nodded. "I've a letter from Philly, and I had a meeting with someone in the Guard in Trellech last night. That's why I was busy. Checking on the laws about public land, and if there was anything specific to say or do if I got stopped."

"You are as thorough as an archaeologist."

It made her blush, and murmur, "Ah, now that's high praise."

Ibis almost didn't feel grumpy. Something about doing this with her felt like an adventure, a joyful one.

She considered, and then reached into the bag, drawing out a cloth knotted around what sounded like buttons, the slip of wood tapping against wood. She drew one out, and he could see they were button blanks, at least, each with a letter on it or a short word. Right. Left. Up. Down. The directions. More. Less.

Ibis blinked at her. "I assume you don't want to change, once we're walking. I thought it might help to have some way to communicate things. I have a vial of paint with me if you think of more."

He shook his head, and then said, "And what did you do in the War, Mrs Gates?"

It earned him a glowing smile. "I figured out solutions to problems." She tucked the bag away. "They're not too big?"

"Not if we're sitting somewhere, and I can show which one. Carrying one would be hard, but flipping it over would be fine."

"There's a cloth with them, so I can just scoop them up if someone comes, it will look like a napkin."

"You seem to have thought of everything."

She went quiet for half a minute, looking out the window, and it wasn't until he said "Pross?" that she turned back to him.

"We still haven't talked about last weekend. What it means."

"We've ..." He consulted his watch. "Half an hour now? Or later, if you'd rather."

"I keep saying later." She paused. "And then doing impulsive things with you."

He was suddenly worried. "Do you regret - did I do something you didn't want?"

Pross shook her head. "Oh, no, no. That's not the problem. The fact I want you to do it again and again, and with rather more variety, that has been very distracting, though." He felt the sudden rush of his blood, and a surge of desire, and she blushed. "Um."

Ibis reached for her hand. "Knowing you want that again, that is ..." He hunted for words. "I want you too. So many ways. Not just in bed, but talking, and ... you keep up with me."

She smiled. "It's just. I know so little about you. A little about your family. And I was clearly not your first lover."

"A few short things, when I was young. A longer one with a woman, when I was posted to Egypt, for several years. She's married now, with three children. Four, maybe. I forget when she's due."

"You're still in touch?"

"Mother is. Mariam is very practical. They have a spice stall. It was her father's. Her husband was injured in the

War. She does much of the work. Ummi sees her at least once a week." He slipped into the familiar name.

"Do you have other family there? Besides your mother and all?"

"They're talking to Ummi again, so yes. Dozens of aunts and uncles and cousins. She's a charm specialist, making protective talismans. You know the tourist things, the protective eyes?"

She nodded.

"Ummi makes ones that actually work. She and Father worked out new techniques. If the family wanted to benefit from the business, they had to talk to her."

"It seems your mother is also brilliant." Pross paused. "Will you - tell her about me?" Her voice turned painfully uncertain.

"Oh, yes. I haven't yet, I wanted to see how we settled out. If you had questions to ask her or wanted to send a note, you'd be welcome. But I write every week, and she'll be back here when Hypatia leaves school, for a party, and to sign the apprenticeship documents formally, and all that." He suspected she didn't mind the fact that was a year away. "Your daughter?"

"I haven't told her anything yet. We talked a little after you stayed. She was tangled up about something with a friend and having you turn up out of the blue didn't help. I haven't told her we spent the night together, but..." Pross paused. "I told her I thought you were interesting. And that I wanted to make sure you knew you were welcome."

"I don't want to ... I'm not sure I'm ready to be a father." It came out hesitantly.

"Not to a teenager. That seems like taking a lot on." There she was being practical again. "There are plenty of ways to be family without that."

"Is that what you want? Family?"

Pross nodded. "You're clever and you're thoughtful and the part in bed was extremely promising. But most of all, you're kind. And you take care of people, your people."

There wasn't much he could say to that. Instead he ventured to settle an arm around her shoulders, and they sat like that until the train pulled into Norwich Station.

TWENTY-NINE

NEAR NORWICH

The plan seemed to go smoothly once they arrived in Norwich. They left the train station together, walked down the main road, parted ways at a crossroad, and she kept walking down toward Philly's family's lands. Ibis took another route out of town, and they met up on a country lane. She'd been waiting a minute or two, long enough to remember to put the maps in an outer pocket for easy reference, and make the minor adjustments that always emerged ten minutes into a walk.

"Have you seen anyone?" Ibis was breathless, as his route had been longer.

Pross shook her head. "Ready?"

There was that moment of his entire body being out of focus, and then there was a hedgehog, snuffling for a moment in the grass. She bent down, not quite kneeling, and held out her hand, letting him climb on, then lifted him to settle in the hammock she'd set up in the knapsack. To her relief, he fit comfortably, it didn't sag out of shape, and she murmured. "Let me try the flap, now."

It took three tries to figure out the best arrangement,

and a few of the button blanks, but they worked out how to fasten it. All of that done, Pross took a deep breath, and set off. Another mile to Caistor St Edmund, the nearest magical village. If all went well, she could take a portal back from there. She tried not to think about if something went wrong. That was asking for trouble.

She paused at the inn to ask for directions. The Guard she'd talked to last night had suggested that, to show she wasn't sneaking around. The pub was getting busy, there was a market day down the street, and she had to wait for a couple of minutes.

"Ma'am?" The question jolted her out of her thoughts.

"Morning. Could I get a bottle of squash to take with me and a hand with directions? I'm looking for Provender, the old Tipson estate. I'm working on a project for Philly." She kept her voice casual. She'd done tasks like this before, but it had been years since she'd had to so balance what she said and how she said it.

"Ah, there's not much there. Well, t'house is still standing." He bustled around. "We've lime, elderflower, or blackberry."

"It's the grounds we're interested in. Oh, elderflower sounds grand. Is it this road, or did I get turned around?" She did her best to sound harmless.

"Aye, take a right out the door, down the road. Should be fine walking on the road, we've not so many cars down there yet, but keep an eye out."

"Dogs or bulls I should keep an eye out for? I've her permission, mind, but I don't intend to get much off the paths." A woman came out of the kitchen, drying off her hands on her apron. "Know about country ways, then?"

"I live in the New Forest, but I know our ways are different."

"Cows and sheep and pigs and ponies and all sorts of things roaming free, I should say so." Pross couldn't figure out if she thought this was horrible or innovative. Though a custom of nearly a millennium could scarcely be called innovative anymore. "Close any gate you open. No bulls this side of Provender, but old man Kitson has a big dog. Black and unfriendly. He's caretaker."

The pub owner coughed, and said, "Might want to have a word with the Guard, ma'am. Since you've permission and all. They've had to run a couple of people off, the last few months. Might save yourself trouble. He should be out on the street, for the market." He finished making up a bottle of squash for her.

"Oh, really? I didn't know there was much interest in the place."

The pub owner settled the bottle in front of her. "Here you go, ma'am. Two soldi, and you get five pence back if you return the bottle."

"Ta, this looks great. I packed lunch, but a cool drink is so much better. I appreciate your help."

With that, she made her way back out the door, and found the Guard quickly. He did not like the idea she had permission much at all and he was gruff with her. But she showed him Philly's letter, promised not to go into the house, and repeated that she expected to stay on the public paths.

The walk to Provender was about as promised. Two miles down a country lane, no particular hills, and easy going. She made it to the first planned stop in good time. Once she found the angle they'd discussed, she set the bag down carefully, and opened the top flap, murmuring, "No one around so far. Time for me to get the watercolours out."

She leaned the bag against a rock, so he could get in and

out, then settled down on another, doing a sketch of the landscape. She began by pencilling in various notable landmarks, careful to get the perspective as close to right as she could, then adding the wash of colour with the paints. She found it soothing, despite her apprehension about what might happen with this plan.

Thirty minutes later, she'd drunk half the bottle of squash, and they were ready to go on to the next point, which was nearer the house. Getting there was fine, and brought them along a stunning line of paired trees, leading up the old drive toward the house. Where the drive continued to the top of the hill and the house itself, she continued to the right, toward the rim of trees around the grounds.

She felt trouble before she either saw it or heard Ibis's agitated scrabbling in the bag. A moment later, there was the sound of footsteps behind her, and the rattling of rings on a dog's collar. She took a breath, and turned around, to face the person coming down the path.

"Oi, this is private property. Clear out!"

She stood her ground. "I've Philly Tipson's permission to be here. I've been keeping to the public paths. Is there a problem?" She'd try sincere questions first.

The man she was facing was in his fifties, and still very active by the looks of him. The dog was indeed black and rather unpleasant looking, a good bit of mastiff in him, big and bulky. She could see why Ibis had worried about the teeth. There were a lot on display.

The fact she had permission clearly gave the caretaker a little pause, and he came closer, saying "Anyone could say that, ma'am." It was at least a little more cautious.

She moved the pack to one arm, to draw out the permission letter tucked behind the maps. "Here. I brought a letter." He took it, and she realised quickly that he had trouble reading it. The dog sniffed around the bottom of her pack.

"Heel your dog." It came out in the kind of command voice she'd heard her parents and their friends use and hated herself. Here, though, it did some good, and the man grudgingly called his dog to sit.

"You have anything in your bag?"

"A sandwich or two." Her voice was sharp, still. "If you doubt the letter, I stopped at the inn in Caistor St Edmund, and spoke to the Guard there, too."

This put him in a quandary. "Still don't know as I should..."

She spoke over him. "I don't intend to go any closer to the house. I'm helping Philly with a project, and I need to know the landscape." There, that description might as easily describe a horticultural project or finding a rare plant, as finding a lost treasure hoard.

He grumbled, and she waited him out. After nearly a minute, he nodded. "No closer to the house. Bull won't like it." He indicated the dog with a sharp nod filled with unpleasant implications.

"I'm planning here, down the path there, then cut across here, back to the main road. Sketching and painting, I'll be gone by four or so."

"See you are, ma'am." It was gruff, but he finally turned away.

She watched him go back up the hill toward the house, and a small cottage by the arched stone and metal gate. Only when he was well out of view did she let out a full breath, then settle the pack on her back again, and keep walking. She could see why Ibis had had a hard time. Without permission and a bit of social manipulation to back him up, and looking as he did, they'd not have given him any grace.

The second stop went smoothly, then the third, and she noted a few details of the way the land curved. There was a hollow that didn't show on the maps, something that might be a deliberate pile of stones, a small mound. All promising.

It wasn't until she was on her way out she had more trouble. She was in the lane, walking back toward the main road, when a man in a sharply tailored tweed suit with a shotgun came along in the other direction. She forced herself to keep walking forward.

"Good afternoon." Again, she would try being pleasant first.

"Private land, here." The man was sharp.

"I've Philly Tipson's permission, I'm working on a project for her, had to see the land for myself."

"Oh?" And then the man seemed to remember his manners. "I'm Theron Davis. I've a small house a mile or two that way. I come along here to keep the vermin down, get a rabbit now and then."

She offered the kind of pleasant smile she'd learned often worked to disarm people. "Kind of you to keep an eye around the place. I met the caretaker, earlier. It will be good to tell Philly people are making sure nothing goes wrong."

He offered back a smile. "How is she doing?"

"You know about her chickens, I'm sure? They're doing very well, she has new chicks keeping her busy." Then she glanced at the sky, then at her watch. "Goodness, if I want to get back at a reasonable time, I should head along."

"Here, let me walk you down to the road." She couldn't put him off without seeming suspicious, so she nodded. She'd hoped for one more sketch from the path, but they'd have to do without.

The conversation was inane, too. About the country, about the village, about how he was an author. Not one she'd ever heard of, mind you, though all she said about that is "Do you have a card on you? I have a small bookshop, nothing fancy, but I do keep an eye out for things to get or recommend."

When they parted at the road, she tucked the card into her pocket. She made her way back as briskly as she could manage to the village, and then to the portal, going back to London.

THIRTY

LONDON

I bis was frustrated. They hadn't been able to talk once they got back to London. Pross had needed to get back to take care of the bookshop in the morning.

It left Ibis with pleasant but unrestful dreams, and in something of a mood on Monday morning. He tried not to take his prickliness out on Jonas, but that involved leaving the house even earlier than usual. Walking to the Research Society, he wondered if naming how he felt as prickly felt better or worse. And of course her comments brought out the perennial question of how much his form revealed about him.

He had been at his desk for a good half hour when there was a knock on his door. It was still quite early, only half-eight, much earlier than he expected anyone to be around.

"Hello?" Maybe it was Pross. He half stood up.

The door opened, but the woman who came in was decidedly not Pross. She was broadly built, likely in her sixties, and one of the senior members who had not been much in evidence in his time there.

"Ward?"

He nodded, standing up the rest of the way, and saying, "Mistress... Newton, isn't it?"

She nodded. "Wenna Newton, yes."

"I'm afraid I don't remember your speciality?"

She eyed him up and down, and said, "If you were in my specialty, you'd be earning high marks for good manners, and possibly not drowning in the greenwood."

He blinked and then ventured, "Folklore?"

"Folk song, to be precise, yes. May I?" She gestured at the chair, closing the door behind her. He nodded and sat down in his own.

"I didn't expect anyone this morning."

"The current residents do not wander in here very early. I admit, it's early for me, too."

Ibis didn't know what to say to that, so he said nothing.

She looked him up and down, and then continued, "You've kicked up some sort of nest, you realise. They're all buzzing with it."

"Ma'am?" He would be polite. It seemed the only way through.

Wenna watched him for a long moment. "They don't like you."

"Ma'am?" Ibis repeated it.

"I believe that makes us allies. Or at least, worth a conversation about it."

"There are plenty of people who don't like me. It has not resulted in a lot of allies to date." He tried to keep his voice neutral, but a bit of bitterness came out despite himself.

She settled back, steepling her hands. "Oh, plenty of reasons for that. You show them up with your work ethic and your ethics. Did you ask questions they found difficult to answer about why there are so few items out? Few people apparently doing any work?"

"No, ma'am. It seemed unwise."

"But you were thinking them?"

Ibis nodded, warily. He did rather feel like he'd wandered into a folk song with a baffling figure speaking in riddles. Drowning, still decidedly a possibility, but lying was not the way through. He was utterly sure this woman would know if he did.

"I gather you're working on this project with someone else?"

Ibis swallowed, and then said, carefully, "Yes, ma'am. Is it necessary to reveal who?"

"Protective of her, are you?" She looked him up and down, and Ibis was certain, down to his bones, that she was evaluating their sex life as part of her examination.

"I am, yes. And this isn't her fight."

Wenna raised an eyebrow. "The Society? Or research?"

"The Society."

"How did she come to bring the question here?"

"Her husband was a fellow, before the War, and a member until his death. Half a dozen years ago."

Wenna clucked her tongue, her eyes half closing. "That would make her Proserpina Gates, then. No one else quite fits. Though we lost too many to the War."

"Ma'am." He paused, then asked, "What are you hoping for?"

She looked him up and down and then said, "I have reasons for not getting too deeply involved. But I wish to know what you know."

Ibis could feel his hackles rising, or whatever the term was. "Ma'am. I will grant we may have a common cause.

But I am not at your beck and call, nor inclined to turn over what information I have on your say so."

That earned him a broad laugh. "Oh, there's a bit of spirit." She tapped her fingers on his desk, and he resented the sound. "I mean you no harm. I am one among others concerned for the future of the Society. I am, we are, curious about what you, a relative newcomer, but observant scholar, might have observed."

Ibis let out a breath, then glanced at the baboon on the corner of his desk, and reached for it and a shallow fired pottery bowl. He uncorked the top of the baboon's head, and poured out ink into the dish, cupping his hands around it. Then he breathed out on it, murmuring the string of prayers and chants his mother had first taught him so long ago.

It was a simple form of divination, but most potent. In times like this, where he had no idea what the correct answer was, it seemed best. The images he got from the ink, or the dance of his mind and the ink, rather, were murky at first, then sharpened.

The images began with a flash of the serpent creature, the sirrush, then something made of faience, flying through the air, he couldn't quite make out the shape. Finally, the images settled into a feather. He made a frustrated noise, deep in his throat, but thanked the gods, with a small prayer under his breath.

He looked up to find Wenna watching him intently, her hands folded in her lap. It was the look in her eyes that made him realise what the symbols meant.

"There is an injustice here. An important one." He paused, and then said, "You have found yourself in a stalemate, that there is no way forward, two equal forces pressing against each other, preventing movement. It is not that you do not wish to be deeply involved, it is that you are stuck."

She raised an eyebrow, paused, then nodded her head.

"And you are curious about me, because I am something different."

This made her laugh again. "Thoughtful and quick-witted. Come on, will you tell us?"

"That depends." He settled back in his chair, gathering all the little tricks of someone of equal status in his body language. It was something he rarely did in England, because it often made his life more difficult, but here he was certain it was necessary. And, perhaps, he might venture that it might possibly even be welcome. Given her praise of him showing spirit.

So he moved: the shift of his shoulders to take up space rather than defer. Looking directly at her eyes, holding his gaze, letting his breath drop in his chest. "What do you and your fellows want?"

"We want the Society to be rebuilt, for study and research, not for personal benefit. There are not so many of us as there were, and we are in less fashionable fields, ones with fewer influential patrons. Fewer resources, on the whole."

Ibis arched an eyebrow. "I am not likely to help you there."

"No, but you may see a different way out of the puzzle that we have not. And I am intrigued by your collaboration."

Ibis inhaled, and then said, "Here, then. I am indeed working with Proserpina Gates. Someone asked her to research a possible lost Roman hoard in Norfolk, on lands held by her client. I went to view the space and was run off. She and I did more archival research, then..."

He tried to figure out how to phrase this so it was not a lie but did not give away how he had been there. "Then there was a further visit, yesterday. We have not yet discussed the specifics."

"Do you know what is in the hoard?"

"Indications from our research suggest that there is a Roman hoard, but that it may contain items from other cultures, possibly Mesopotamian. There's a word used in one reference that suggests something barbarian - not Roman, not Greek, made of stone."

"And you think that's what the other party is interested in?"

"It seems plausible. We're unlikely to know for sure without an actual excavation."

"What would you need to make that happen?"

Ibis frowned. "I don't know yet if we have a location determined. Pross made watercolours and sketches of the various locations yesterday, but we will need to compare them to maps and our notes. You understand, the stories are spread across a millennia or so, and have varying levels of specificity."

Wenna nodded. "Granted. But when you have done that, what do you need?"

"Ideally, trained archaeologists. Barring that - oh, interested students with shovels, trowels, and ability to follow directions. Supplies to support them, food and drink. Equipment to record the site, paper and photography equipment."

Wenna nodded. "You've done this before. Run a dig."

Ibis nodded. No false modesty here. "Not in Albion, but yes." he agrees.

"How long would it take?"

Ibis frowned. "It depends on the site. A week or two for

initial evaluation. If we found something we could narrow down quickly. Hoards are normally tightly clustered. There are some magical tools we may apply. A tool for echoing sympathetic magic, for example."

Wenna nodded. "Send me a list of what you will need, and what other items would be helpful. We'll have them ready." Then, she stood up. "A most interesting conversation, Ward."

THIRTY-ONE

TRUE EYEWORTH

"I missed you."

Pross refrained from flinging herself at him. It had been a week since she'd seen him, and she hadn't been able to get away to London. She held out her arms to him, and he set down his overnight bag and stepped into them, kissing her at once.

His notes during the week had been quite brief, limited to the practicalities.

As he stepped back, she could see he finally took in the room. There were sizeable sheets of paper tacked on the walls, and several large boards with more sheets propped against the kitchen table.

"Have you taken up architecture?"

"Maps." Pross was cheerful. "I spent a bit of time with Geoffrey's library this week, since I couldn't get away to see you." It was now Saturday, a week after their expedition.

"Do you need to be downstairs, for the shop?" He sounded like he was worried she was neglecting it. "I have a lot to catch you up about, but it can wait until you close."

"One of the village girls is minding it. We don't get a lot

of business on market day, but she'll let me know if there's anything that needs me in person."

"I just, I know it's important to you."

That warmed her and earned him another kiss. "Put your bag down. There's a little table there, for taking notes. Tea? Scones? Something more substantial?"

He laughed and said, "I had breakfast before I left. Lord Carillon sends his regards, he was in the courtyard when I came through."

She beamed. "Was he working with the black mare, or a different one?"

"A grey, this time. Tea would be good. Let me look at these before I sit down? Where should I start?"

"That is a sketch of the property, marking the most likely locations. Then detailed maps of the four possibilities, with the historical map as a tracing paper overlay on the current ordnance map. Then, there, those are the sketches and watercolours I did when we were there, and then I made duplicates."

He blinked at her. "The duplication magic isn't easy. Especially not with art. Nicely done."

Pross laughed and said, "One of my hidden talents. I use it for many of my circulars and advertising." She said it lightly, but the way he said it, that helped a lot.

The lack of communication had troubled her. She couldn't tell if the brief messages he'd sent were him being busy. Or was he feeling she wasn't holding up her side of the work, or were there security issues, worries about someone finding out what he wrote. She had worried if it had been a security concern that asking would have been the absolute worst thing to do.

Which meant she'd spent the better part of a week trying to talk away the whirring intrusive thoughts of not being good enough or smart enough or knowledgeable enough, or skilled enough. It wasn't like her fears didn't have material to work with.

He'd mastered shape-shifting, a complex magic, he had research and language abilities she could only dream of. But no, here he was, treating her like an equal.

He smiled at her and then focused his attention on the boards and sketches. She watched him, not wanting to turn away. Tea was required, so she finally busied herself with that, setting the kettle to boil, measuring out her own. "Do you want mint again?"

He nodded, absently, leaning in to look at a juxtaposition between one of the historical maps and the modern one.

"There's a thing I want to talk through with you," she added. He nodded again, that absent look of a researcher deep in conversation with his sources, and she smiled at the back of his head.

He took a good half hour to look at everything. He didn't rush, he didn't skim, he gave it all serious attention. Finally, when she'd put the kettle on to boil for a third time, he turned to face her. "This is fantastic. A good copyist is essential for an excavation. You have a lovely hand with it, and the way you've indicated the possible changes."

It was grand to be attractive to him physically, and she knew now she was. But she loved this even more, watching his eyes light up and glow. She'd seen glimpses, before, but this was stronger, it lasted longer.

She let out a breath. "I wasn't sure if I was overstepping. Or making assumptions not supported by the evidence."

He shook his head. "I want to work through a few of your suppositions. Those last three boards, the one where you were applying material in the records, what they might mean. I think I agree, but we should talk through it more."

Pross nodded, and fussed with the tea, before bringing it over. She considered her worries, then said "I feel like I'm about to be marked. Which is silly, I know."

He took it seriously. "I know things you don't. You know things I don't. That's how research is supposed to work, we can't all be the expert at everything. So. Tell me why you think that third site is the one."

Pross took a breath, settling herself. "You remember that comment in the record from 1291? About how it wasn't touched by the flood? I got to thinking about what that meant. If it had flooded, and there was a hoard, then pieces might have washed out. I know you had a theory it might be protected magically."

"That part is sound, yes. But that also applies here, with the flooding in 1465." He gestured at the second location.

"This will sound odd, but... sketching it. The second site wanted me to look at it. The third site didn't. Like it was trying to hide."

Ibis tilted his head, then nodded. "I didn't get as good a look." He tapped his fingers on the mug he was holding. "What about the last one, the one you didn't have time to do much with?"

"I remain suspicious about Theron Davis. I thought he turned up awfully conveniently."

"Hiding something about the site? In league with the rather distasteful caretaker?"

"Oh, I have news about that, too. The caretaker is a woman, I asked Philly. The man is apparently a nephew or cousin or something of hers who helps with the heavy work, but he's not supposed to live on the property."

Ibis raised an eyebrow. "No one else is."

"I gather he's got a disreputable reputation. Not a bad War, something before that. I found a few newspaper references, about a trial, but what I had was only about the appeal, and it didn't have details."

Ibis shook his head. "I did not like him. Nor his dog."

"I do see why you ran." Pross agreed.

"The bag worked very well. And your clever invention, even better. Did I say that enough, last week?"

She smiled at him. "You can keep saying it. And it was really useful. There are risks to being a woman out on your own, but there are also a lot of people who think you have to be entirely harmless."

He tilted his head, watching her, and she admitted, "I did a bit of that in the War. Nothing terribly dangerous, but message drops, a few times. Observing people, who wouldn't suspect I was anything other than a mother out with a pram or a little one."

"Oh, no, decidedly not." Ibis asked, after a moment's thought, "Does Cammie know she helped her parents with official business as a baby?"

"That is a story for when she's an adult, and won't spread it around school."

"Ah, very sensible." Ibis agreed. Then, carefully, a "Did you want other children?" He'd clearly been trying to find a chance to ask it.

Pross shrugged. "A bit. It didn't happen."

Ibis coughed, and said, "That was, I suppose, more of a personal inquiry, and a general one. Seeing as how..."

She blinked. "Oh. Um. Yes." She considered, and then said, "I'm young enough yet I could try again, though I'd want to have a long conversation with a Healer, first. But I don't..."

She stopped, swallowing, before she continued. "Cammie's lovely, and if that's the child I have, that is fine. So it'd be a thing we could talk about. Depending on what you wanted. And sometimes children don't happen, even when they're wanted and you're trying."

He nodded, but didn't reply, as if he was thinking through what to say.

She took a breath. "I took precautions, last time. And - I mean, I rather hope tonight is on offer, at the least. Because children is a more complicated conversation. Not one I want to be spontaneous about."

The last sentence made him laugh and say, "Don't tie yourself in knots. I know Ummi would like me to have children. But I haven't been able to figure out if I like the idea of it, or would like the reality, you know? But you're right, that's a longer and larger conversation. Knowing you're open to either direction, that's a kind thing to tell me now."

Pross flushed. "Kind's an odd way to put it."

Ibis shrugged. "A lot of people would want it their way. Or not think about the future."

Pross nodded. "It's complicated. I wrote to my parents that I was seeing someone. That you'd worked in the Colonial Service, that you were Anglo-Egyptian."

"Will that be a problem for them?"

Pross shrugged. "Maybe. Octavian was mixed, half his family's from Africa, by way of Italy. You've seen Cammie, it shows in her, too. But he was First Families, quite a long way back." She paused, then added, "Though your father was quite respectable, by Papa's standards."

That made Ibis smile. "That's something. What counts as respectable?"

"He took care of his people and lived up to his responsibilities. Didn't shirk, didn't get tangled in scandal. Papa's very much live and let live about people who keep their private lives private. I don't think you can spend long in the Colonial Service as a decent person without sorting out how you feel about people who make very different choices than you'd make. But he hates fuss and people being dramatically wronged all over the place and dragging him out of bed at all hours to fix things."

Ibis laughed. "That seems quite reasonable." Then he turned and looked at the sketches. "I think our next step is to work out an excavation plan for that third site, so I we can figure out workers and tools."

"Geoffrey said he'd help, he knows some people."

THIRTY-TWO

SCHOLA

The meeting felt oddly reminiscent of the War. There were six people gathered in a well-appointed room, some sitting, some standing. Old leather-bound books lined the shelves, and the large table in the centre was covered in maps and sketches, with others on the easels around the room.

This time, however, the windows did not look out on Cairo, or London, but on the Schola courtyard. It was a Sunday; the students were otherwise occupied. Richart came in, escorting the last arrival, a young dark-haired man who clearly felt out of his depth. "Tea and scones there, do keep them away from the papers."

Pross had settled, a little out of the way, in one chair. Ibis circled the room to come and stand behind her, resting a hand on the back of the chair, his finger just brushing the back of her shoulder. The others in the room took their time in settling down, but eventually everyone had a chair, and everyone had a notebook out.

Ibis stepped forward. "Thank you all for taking time to consult on this challenge, and for being willing to come here to accommodate Master Richart Hase, who cannot leave school during term. Our plan for today is to discuss and come up with an initial plan. We will then present it to Amphyllis Tipson, Philly, who can grant permission for the dig we would like to undertake.

He shifted, then continued. "We should take a moment for introductions. I am Ibis Ward, a fellow of the Research Society, and Pross brought the problem at hand to my attention. My research focuses on Egypt, but I do have experience managing a full archaeological dig, and assisted with a significant portion of the research for this project thus far."

Pross stood at this, and said "I am Proserpina Gates - do call me Pross, please. I'm a bookseller and researcher based in the New Forest. Philly came to me for advice on locating the Roman hoard long rumoured to be buried on her family land near Norwich. I did the initial research in records and then have consulted with Ibis about how to narrow down likely locations."

Richart nodded from his seat. "Richart Hase, Head of Seal House, here at Schola. Ibis and Pross consulted me about this matter, in the hopes I could suggest lines of research. I've also made available a few items from our library collection. They may not leave this room, but are available for consultation."

That left Ibis to nod at Wenna, who inclined her head. "I am Wenna Newton, a senior member of the Research Society. My speciality is not relevant here, as it related to folk song. I am here with my associate representing those members of the Society interested in practical hands-on research. I expect to facilitate access to certain resources."

Her companion, an older man who rather resembled a raven, between the black coat, black hair, and the narrowness of his head and shape of his nose nodded. "Bertram

Tipson. I happen to be a relative of Philly's and am also a senior member of the Research Society. I have extensive materia expertise, but am not suited for fieldwork these days." He gestured at an elegant cane propped against the table beside him.

The youngest man there had waited patiently and nodded to the others. "Good afternoon. I am Farran Michaels, a materia specialist with one of the auction houses, finishing my apprenticeship. Lord and Lady Carillon suggested my skills might be of use in locating the hoard once initial sounding pits were made or assisting in evaluating items found."

Wenna raised an eyebrow at the invocation of the names. Pross said, "They've been quite helpful - they hold Ytene, so I knew them through that, but they're both enthusiastic readers. They've made several useful suggestions."

Ibis smiled at her, and then said, "Our thought was that we'd present the current proposal to you, see if there were any concerns. And then write it up for Philly Tipson."

Bertram tapped his fingers, and said, "Michaels, which auction house are you with?"

"Ormulu, sir. I am senior apprentice under Master Ettis." He paused for a moment. "Master Philemon Ettis."

That clearly startled Bertram, who nodded, and said, "I know him quite well," before adding, "We should be on first names here, I think."

Richart snorted, and said, "As you say, Bertram." He gestured to Ibis and Pross together. "Would you walk us through the plan?"

They had rehearsed this several times, and Ibis rose, focusing on looking unhurried and at ease. Their calm and certainty would help make their case. If they were going to convince Philly, and convince Wenna and Bertram to offer

more support, he and Pross had to look like they were confident in their success. He carried one easel over beside them.

"Because of the security concerns, we are cautious
about releasing this material. It seemed best to walk through
the extant information, and then identify the sites we
believe most promising."

It was Bertram who spoke up again. "Sites? I thought
you proposed to investigate a specific site. And what security concerns are these?"

Pross came up to the other side of the easel. "We have
narrowed down the location to two particular areas of the
property."

It was Wenna who asked what they'd only realised last
night would come up. "Why are you so certain the site is on
that property? Surely the boundaries of their land have
changed."

Pross smiled. "Less than in many places, and many of
the changes are because of geographic changes - the river,
here, changed course."

She tapped the easel with her hand, a particular
pattern, and the river shifted into colour. "This is the line
before the 1290 flood. This is the line after, and then you
can see as it progresses, how this curve here deepen, and
this becomes more shallow." She tapped her finger each
time, showing the changes.

Wenna leaned forward, looking at the shifts, then
nodded. "You've thought this through." she agreed. "Why
those two sites?" She was relentless, rather like a terrier.

Ibis took half a step back, then turned to the table,
bringing around packets of copied material. "These are the
initial texts we worked with, and translations. Using these
materials, we narrowed it down to four likely sites. That is
based on the description of the hoard being buried below

the top of the hill and ridge line, in a field, and adjusting for the historic shift of field to forest to field. We suspected that if the hoard were here or here...."

He indicated two spots on the map, "Someone would have been found already: these fields were both ploughed over the centuries."

"Why the two sites, then?"

"Pross took a trip to do the sketches, here, let me bring those closer." As he did so, Pross picked up.

"You can see in the sketch here, some particular white flowers. I wasn't able to get a close look at them at the time, but we realised afterwards that they are likely Enchanter's Nightshade."

It was Farran who spoke, then. "Those are a particular indicator of materia in the soil. It's not entirely reliable, of course, but I agree it would suggest a site worth more attention."

Bertram asked, "Why did you not investigate more closely?"

Pross shifted back on her heels, and Ibis came back beside her. "I made an initial investigation, staying entirely on public paths, and was run off. When Pross went, she took care to make it clear she had permission."

"I still had a rather unpleasant encounter with someone who claimed to be the caretaker. According to Philly, he isn't. And then, I met by someone who claims to be living nearby, and keeping an eye on the property. He is a recent arrival in the area, as far as we can tell."

Richart coughed. "You investigated?"

"It seemed curious. It's hard to tell right now what is going on, but there are signs that some party or parties wants what is in the hoard for some reason. Logic says it is possible that Philly has withheld information, or that one or

more of the other parties we have met is lying or misrepre-
senting their role. That's why I want to present a complete
proposal to Philly, and to take the next step in company."

Wenna chewed on that for a minute. "What is supposed
to be in the hoard?"

Ibis replied, "The hoards found so far have a mix of
coins, objects, and sometimes other items. Cups, plates,
jewellery are all common, and in a hoard from a magical
family, magical items are quite possible."

Then, he glanced at Pross. They'd discussed how much
of this to reveal, but this was the most delicate part. "There
are hints that the item of particular interest may be stone,
and Mesopotamian. There are rumours, associated with
Roman families in the area, of a cylinder seal associated
with Marduk. We've only been able to do the most cursory
research on that aspect so far, but it's possible that such an
item would have particular materia properties."

"That's why you wanted someone with materia skill?"
That was Ferran again.

Ibis nodded. "My own skills aren't bad, but they're not
suited to what we'll find, or the environment, so we wanted
more than one approach available."

Ferran inhaled, looking back, and almost said something. Ibis wondered for a split second whether this would
be an unfortunate conversation, or whether the young man
would avoid it. When Ferran spoke, he said, "May I ask
your own training, Ibis, to compliment it?"

It was rather better than Ibis had expected. "I trained
under a number of archaeologists, both magical and otherwise, in Egypt. I can give you a copy of my curriculum vitae
if you wish. My training in materia was familial, on my
mother's side - Egyptian techniques not regularly taught

here. If you find them promising, I would gladly offer a lecture at Ormulo, of course, as a thank you for your help."

He paused, considered, then continued. "The approach I learned relies on sympathetic magics, rather than resonance. While they are quite effective for finding a specific material, in the case of locating a possibly mythical cylinder of unknown stone, a resonance approach may prove more successful. I know the theory, but have had little chance to refine the skill myself."

It was lengthy, but he hoped very much it would satisfy the younger man's standard. Out of the corner of his eye, he glimpsed Richart nodding. Ibis let out a breath. Now they could settle into the details of how many people might be needed or useful, what equipment and tools, and how to present the whole process to Philly.

THIRTY-THREE

NEAR NORWICH

It took the entire next week to get everything organised. Pross felt she'd had a pen in her hand for days on end, tracking comments from different people, confirming tools and resources and people who would turn up. It was at least the Floralia break at Schola, which allowed Richart to join them.

Philly, at least, had been easy to convince. It had only taken them walking through the proposal for her to nod at it, and say, "That's why I hired you, to come up with a sensible plan. When do I turn up? I can bring my own shovel."

Explaining that the shovel was not the ideal tool for excavation had taken rather longer than her initial agreement. Ibis had been tremendously patient, Pross thought.

Now, here they were, with mist rising off the grass. Ibis came up beside her and murmured, "Ready?"

"Ready as we're going to be. Half a dozen young men with relevant skills over here. People with materia expertise over there. People with strong and not always informed opinions sitting down and having tea." That last was Philly.

"What does that make us, then?"

Pross snorted. "Theoretically responsible?"

"Only theoretically? That's promising. I was always rather good at theory."

It made Pross laugh before she said, "We'll see if someone shows up to throw fits." They'd taken appropriate precautions on that front, alerting the local Guard, and bringing another with them, in case anything turned up in the excavation that needed immediate protection.

Ibis nodded, and said, "Let me get things started, then." He went off to do that, leaving Pross standing on a ridge overlooking both their potential sites. They would do a trial sounding in both places, so they could deploy two magical devices that might offer a more definitive answer. Pross settled into the camp chair, and started work on some of the sketches and notes they'd need later.

Pross felt the hairs on the back of her neck stand up before she heard anything, but then there was a low growl of the dog, and a shout. "Oy, this is private property."

She and Ibis had talked about what to do if this happened. She rose, turned, and said "We have the permission of the family." One of the helpful young men came up to her, at the shout and Pross murmured, "Can you fetch Philly Tipson, please? The woman in the hat, down there."

Then she turned, to face the man who claimed to be the caretaker, and summoned all her patience and fortitude to remain there, quiet. Not letting him see she was nervous. Not giving anything away.

She heard Philly come up behind her. "What's all this?"

"Philly, this is the man I mentioned from the last visit."

Philly looked him up and down. "Jacob Waters." Her voice was very sharp, much sharper than Pross had ever heard her.

It earned her a grudging, "Ma'am."

"Family land, I'm here to oversee. What are you doing?"

"Keeping an eye on the place, ma'am."

"And if I asked your ma what you are doing?"

The man took a step back. Something in him was utterly cowed, where a minute ago he'd been bluster and entirely in control.

Philly leapt at that. "Right. Guard!"

It took a bit of time for the Guard to make it up the hill. "Guardsman, this is the son of the actual caretaker. Can you summon someone else, to keep an eye here, while we go make sure she's all right and aware of what's going on?"

It was apparently not the question the Guard was expecting, but after a moment of parsing it, he nodded. "Ma'am," he agreed, and turned away, writing something in a small notebook. "They'll have to come down from the portal in Caistor St Edmund, ma'am, but there'll be a horse at the station there, it shouldn't take too long."

Philly nodded, eyeing the dog, who had subsided into the occasional growl. "You stay right there until the Guard arrives. Prossie, dear, you go see about the excavation."

Pross did so, quite promptly, coming down the hill to find Ibis, and murmur, "Philly is staring down the nasty man with the big dog. We've got another of the Guard coming. Want to make a bet on whether we see the too helpful Theron Davis in the next half an hour?"

Ibis laughed and said, "I'll take forty-five minutes or longer."

"Done."

It was thirty-seven minutes. Ibis looked up, then dug in his pocket to hand over a coin. Philly and the Guard had migrated a little further away, and Pross and Ibis were at the site nearest the road.

"I say, is this... oh, Mrs Gates?"

Pross straightened from where she'd been examining some of the results of the first sounding hole. Farran had been using one of the magical devices to detect signs of materia, and the initial responses were puzzling. She brushed off her hands. "Mr Davis, isn't it?"

"Oh, Theron, please."

She nodded and did not return the invitation. "Is there a problem?"

He blinked at her, all apparent innocence. "This is, you do realise, Mrs Gates, that this is private property?"

"Oh, of course. Philly Tipson, the family representative, is right up there, dealing with another matter."

"But I'd thought..." His voice trailed off.

Pross leaned into the moment. "Did you think someone else was responsible? I gathered, doing some of my research, that someone had implied that. But I checked - that's my role, looking after all the details - that Philly has the right to permit what we're doing here. To be certain we got a signed agreement from her sister and cousin, the other two with the land rights."

Davis looked like a fish for a moment. Then, his eyes narrowed, and he looked at something behind her. "Who's that man, there?"

Pross glanced over her shoulder, and said, "Ibis Ward. He's the supervising archaeologist."

Davis frowned. "Him?"

"He's had significant roles on a number of digs in Egypt, much larger and more complex than this. And of course, we have fewer crocodiles. Though he tells me hippos are more of a danger." She couldn't decide if Davis himself were more hippo or crocodile, or perhaps something else.

She was rewarded with a bit of silence, and she did not invite him to come investigate. While they were there, in their state of detente, she said, "Oh, here's the new Guard, up to help. Excuse me, Mr Davis, I've various matters to see to. We can't accommodate visitors to the site at the moment."

She gestured, behind her back, and then turned to catch Ibis's hand, flashing quickly in the sign that said he'd keep an eye out.

Dealing with the Guard took a good five minutes, and when she finally returned to Ibis, he was frowning over two samples of dirt, on opposite ends of the worktable.

"Any problem?"

"The new Guard - his name is Falstaff, would you believe? - is going off with Philly to check on the actual care-taker. Philly says if anyone else wishes to be difficult before they get back, to form a queue."

"I am beginning to like her humour more than I did." His voice was dry.

"What are you puzzling over?"

"These samples. This is that device Farran mentioned. It should show which sample has had greater proximity to materia." He pointed it first at the sample on the left, then the sample on the right, moving so that there was no cross-effect. Both times, the device lit up with a glow, about the same strength, and made a chime noise of three tones.

"What does that mean?" Pross followed him around, to see the thing from the same angle.

"Well, it means either the device is not calibrated correctly, or that they are equivalent in materia influence. There are more settings you can turn on to refine the read-ings, but I don't know that they'll be helpful yet."

Pross stared at the two samples. Nothing changed, of

course. She came back to settle on the camp chair, then said, carefully. "Is there a way to tell what kind of materia is involved? The raw materials, for example? It seems improbable that we'd have two buried hoards of equivalent magical interest within a quarter mile of each other."

Ibis snorted. "A great deal of archaeology is improbable, but I agree." He tapped the table. "You're on to something with the materials. Let me go get Richart."

Pross shook her head. "In a minute. Which of these came from which test sounding?"

Ibis shook his head. "I don't know. Deliberately, so I can't influence the initial testing."

"Richart, then." It took a minute or two to get him out of a conversation with one of the earnest young men. They explained the problem to him, and Pross's questions.

He frowned at the samples, then said, "How does this work?" and he tested it, once Ibis explained the device. "And the other device?"

"That's directional, once we provide a sample of affected soil, it will direct the holder to where there is a greater concentration."

"Like the children's game, hot and cold." That made Pross laugh.

Ibis was patient for several minutes, through another round of testing. Then he said "Do you have a solution? Or an idea? I admit I'm stuck."

Richart nodded, and then said, "Look, I want to try an experiment. I want you both to walk separately to each of the test sites, and then come back and hold your hands over each sample. See which one pulls more strongly, the quality of the feel. Don't try to rationalise it, I want what you feel, with as little logic in the way as possible."

Pross raised an eyebrow, but she nodded. "If you think it

will help."

"It won't hurt."

Ibis laughed. "Try the non-destructive choice first, yes."

And so they went off, separately, to explore each location.

THIRTY-FOUR

NEAR NORWICH

Ibis was not sure what to expect. He walked through one site, then the other, and he couldn't decide on what he felt. After twenty minutes, he and Pross met up at the work-table, while the young men continued digging a test hole to see if they uncovered any physical evidence.

Richart leaned back. "Well?"

Pross spoke first, glancing at Ibis. "I felt something, but I don't know what to make of it."

Ibis nodded. "Me too."

"How about this," said Richart. "Write it down on these slips of paper, and then I'll read them off."

Pross snorted. "Do you read novels, Richart? Those mysteries where people theorise about the murderer?"

Richart waved a hand. "Write."

They both did. Ibis kept his brief, finishing half a sentence before Pross. They handed the slips over, and then Richart handed them the other's. "Read them aloud, do."

Pross went first. "The east pit feels too cool, like something that shouldn't be there. The west pit feels warm, deliberately inviting."

Ibis snorted at this, and read, "I feel a strong pull to the west pit, like a sense of gravity. And something distancing at the east pit, a space, almost like a moat, something hidden behind walls."

Richart gestured. "And what do you make of that?"

"Something wants us to pay attention to the west pit, and not the east one. That suggests..." Pross considered, chewing on her thoughts. "That suggests that we're more likely to find what we want in the east pit."

"Only, would they have had time to set up two pits?" Ibis wanted to think through the logic. "We have assumed the hoard existed because people couldn't take valuables with them. The cylinder seal would be small, if there is one, so why not just take it? Why take the time to bury it?"

"What do we know about what else might be there?"

"Possibly jewellery, possibly silver or gold coins. Possibly items of magical value..." Ibis considered. "There's a tomb in Egypt, where they found a suggestion of items that were kept separate, because they couldn't be moved easily, without special care. That's a thing someone might bury."

Pross offered, "Ibis, you remember how you asked about water, to put Philly off the track?"

Ibis nodded.

"What if there were a well or cistern or something of the kind? The feeling I got from it was damp and cold. What if they used that initial shape to shield whatever was inside? Water can insulate, magically. That's why Schola is on an island."

Richart leaned forward. "And a well or cistern might have a large amount of stone, which can take protective or disguising magics well. That is an excellent thought, Pross."

"Someone might have created a protected space, in case they needed it. I suppose..." Pross tapped her fingers on the table.

"Sir? Sir?" It was one of the young men. "We found something curious, in the east site. Stone."

Ibis laughed and said, "I have rarely seen an archaeological theory produce evidence quite that promptly."

The three made their way down the hill, to where two of the young men were standing, with Farran supervising. "The device reacted, just as we hit this stone layer. It was a sour sound, discordant. I didn't know it could do that." He sounded half delighted at a new thing to learn about, and half baffled.

"We just came up with a theory that the other site might be a decoy, and this one designed to discourage attempts to explore it."

"Huh." Farran looked thoughtful. "How should we proceed then?"

"Carefully. Both because we don't know how they did this layer of protections, if that's what it is, and because we don't know what else is below it." Ibis was clear on that.

Richart cleared his throat. "Actually, I might suggest a few more experts. Can we keep a watch up here, for a day or two?"

Pross considered. She tilted her head, and Ibis could tell she was sorting through supplies. "We arranged two camping wagons. Just in case, from the village. We'd need to get in a few more supplies, we hadn't expected to use them tonight."

Richart nodded. "How about this, then? How about we leave a few people here, including one of the Guard, with supplies and materials. You do whatever planning you need to do, and I'll arrange the experts, and we'll continue when we've got everything in place."

Pross watched him, her head tilted to one side. "You really do think there's a danger."

"I think it's possible." Richart agreed. "And people live longer when they don't poke the unknown magical item up close."

Ibis shook his head and said, "It's hard to argue with the logic of that." he agreed. "Pross, the coordination would be easier from London, I expect."

Pross nodded. "I'll go see about Philly." she agreed.

It took the better part of two hours to sort everything out, another hour to walk to the portal in Caistor St Edmund. And longer still to collect takeaway and beer and get back to Ibis's flat.

He paused before he sat down, going to the kitchen, and then to the shrine, lighting the incense brazier, then setting incense going, murmuring one of the incantations of thanks. "You don't mind the smell, I hope?" he asked, when he came back to sit down.

Pross shook her head. "It's unfamiliar, but lovely. I'm more used to the Indian incenses."

"Kyphi." Ibis murmured. "Honey, wine, raisins, myrrh, juniper, a variety of others." He let out a long breath and then looked at Pross. "Do you want a bath, before anything else?"

"Food, then bath, then - I presume you don't mind if I stay over?"

"You are entirely welcome in my bed whenever you please." Ibis couldn't resist grinning at her.

"I can't believe we found it."

Ibis shook his head. "I am worried it is too simple. And

I'm worried that the other people after it may make trouble."

"Was that why you were taking to the Guard so long?"

Ibis nodded. "I wanted to explain what might show up. I think they were going to set up warning beacons. I'm most worried about some of the magics to induce sleep."

"Is that a thing?"

"Tomb robbers have used them for millennia." He waved a hand. "Incense is a common method, you don't need a lot of some of them in the air to make people drowsy, or sleep more deeply. Though they'll still wake if there's a nearby significant noise. Keeping someone asleep through an excavation would be harder, but there's a lot you can do in a few minutes."

Pross shook her head. "I'm not entirely used to thinking like that," she admitted.

"It helps if you've planned that kind of thing in your past, I suspect." He let the words slip up, then watched her reaction closely.

"You have, of course." It really wasn't a question. "In the War?"

"And before and since. Rarely, but often enough."

"When you had thumbs, or actually," He could see a thought strike her. "Would you be willing to investigate as a hedgehog?"

He frowned. "I don't want to let other people know."

"Which is complicated when we've got twenty people around," she admitted. "We can keep it in reserve as an idea?"

He nodded, and then took a bite or two of his food, then more. He was famished. When he set his fork down again, she was watching him.

"What do you want after this?"

"I'd like to investigate the interesting artefacts in the Petrie collection, and others. I'd like to write a few papers or a book, or something useful. I want to see Hypatia settled in a career she chooses and can do well in." He glanced away for a moment, then looked back at her. "I'd like to see where things go for us."

"You do realise that involves telling Cammie. Beyond my mentioning it to my parents."

"I defer to you on that point, but I assumed so, yes."

"And the complex skills you don't talk about?"

"It's possible they might get called on again. It's been every year or so. A trip somewhere, doing a specific thing as part of my other activities. Nothing dangerous, on the whole. They'd be upset if I insisted on stopping."

"The kind of upset that would cause difficulties?"

"Yes, rather." His voice turned dry again, and he could see at once that she was getting the meaning he couldn't quite spell out. That it could lead to his other work dropping away.

"Are they allies against the folks in the Society who are being twits?"

That thought struck him as curious. "Why do you ask?"

Pross set down her own fork and curled a foot up under her on the couch. "Some people clearly want the Research Society to be functional. Some people clearly don't, or rather are out to get what they can, without considering the greater good."

"The question is, are they after power, after influence, or after things?"

Pross frowned. "I did more reading about Marduk," she said, after a pause. "There's something very evocative of the British Empire, there, the idea of spreading out and over-whelming the other places it touched. And of course, they framed it as bringing joy and prosperity and civilisation, but we know it's not that simple, that overwriting other people's choices isn't joyful."

"And it's a fragile prosperity. A serpent too big to respond to change, lashing out at anything that threatens it."

"That," she agreed. "We can't take down an empire. We're two people."

"More than two interested in it, love," he murmured, watching how she leaned forward.

"True. But we can do this bit. Not let it get worse."

"So ideally, we'd find some way to disgrace them. Remove that set from grasping for power. And then see what else there was."

"Would your keepers in the Intelligence Service approve?"

Ibis steepled his hands, thinking hard. "My oaths are held by the Silence, and they're about protecting magic, and people with magic. Not, specifically, about the empire."

He could see her work through why. "They predate the empire, of course."

"They're quite old oaths. Back to the early Tudors. It was a different time, with different goals."

"I know other places have their own oaths. But it's always the magic first." She searched for the right words. "The modern nation-state later."

"That." he agreed.

Pross let out a long sigh. "I can do that," she said, utterly relieved. "Support magic. I mean, I want people without magic to be happy and safe and prosperous too? But I don't think that's a problem."

Ibis shook his head. "It's my oath, not yours."

"If we're going to be close, I need to support you

keeping your oath. Not get in the way, or get upset at you for keeping it."

He shook his head. "You're a rare woman, Proserpina." Then he nodded at their discarded dishes. "Bath, and bed? Ladies first."

THIRTY-FIVE

NEAR NORWICH

They spent Tuesday in their own pursuits. Ibis had various items to locate and pack. Pross had made a trip out to Schola, by portal, consulting first with the senior librarian and then with the senior professor for Alchemy both of whom were still in residence despite the holidays.

She'd had to invoke Richart's name, and pass along a note, mind. Pross had been a decent student, and competent enough in her alchemy classes, but she felt she'd always been rather a disappointment to Master Norton. The glues, inks, and paints of the bookbinding world fascinated her, and they were considered not very interesting by most in other fields.

Master Norton had been taken aback at her request, she could see that as soon as she knocked on his office. But she'd been able to explain what she wanted, and he was glad to provide the tools and the workspace she needed. Thankfully, the apothecary in the village had had the supplies.

It baffled her that it was this simple, given all the ways it could be used. Apparently, though, if you could hunt up just one or two odd ingredients, you could make incense to put people to sleep.

Wednesday, they made their way back to the site, through the village. By the time Pross could set her bag down, her shoulders were aching. When they arrived, it seemed that everything was undisturbed. They worked through lunch, getting to a point where they uncovered what was clearly some stone structure, under the hill.

"An old well or cistern, perhaps. Half-ruined and then covered over? It would have made an excellent hiding place, and easier to find again than just digging." Ibis went back to pore over the maps. Richart arrived then, with several more tools for evaluating magical concerns.

They were sitting, having lunch, when Pross was startled to realise both Richart and Ibis were alert. Ibis, in particular, was taking care not to show it. She could see the flash of his eyes, and a quick gesture of his hand, for her to not give anything away. She at once set up a little monologue about what supplies they had, when they'd need to restock food, nothing that anyone overhearing could do much with.

After a few minutes, Richart shook his head, and whispered. "Ibis?"

"I didn't see anything, and yet."

"What did you sense?"

Ibis was about to say something, when one of the young men, a specialist in metals and stones, came over. "Sirs? Ma'am? You said to report anything odd, and I - I don't know what this is."

Ibis nodded. "Go ahead, Piers," he said, easily.

"We were eating lunch over by the east site, and I couldn't see anything, but I heard something like - something slipping over stone? Not stone against stone, that's a different sound."

Pross wasn't sure what to say to this, but Ibis just nodded. "Thank you for reporting that. You let me know if you think you hear anything else, all right?"

Once he was gone, Richart considered, then said, "One device I brought will ensure a bit of privacy. It's obvious if anyone comes close, but may I?"

"A good idea, please." Ibis was tightlipped.

It took several minutes to set the thing up, and it spun, rather distracting Pross from the topic at hand.

Once it was whirring away softly, Richart said, "Do you think that was someone trying to get in?"

"We already suspected Aimtree was a snake shifter." Ibis's voice was a little hard. "I won't take that bet."

Pross considered this, then blinked. "We thought it was dangerous in there. Possibly."

That provoked a round of Ibis swearing, first softly, then louder, in what she thought must be Arabic. It was long, extended, and she suspected possibly profane. He tapered off into silence, finally, then looked up. His eyes were flashing as if he expected someone to make a comment.

Richart held his hands up, and Pross murmured, "Not fond of the idea of saving him from his idiocy?"

That earned her a dry, "No. Nor the idea of going in there unprepared."

Richart murmured, "Let me give you two a chance to talk, while I stretch my legs. I'll be back in, oh, ten minutes."

Pross let him go, and then held out a bottle of lemonade to Ibis, carefully. He stretched, then said. "I don't like this."

"I don't either. But we do want to know what's in there, and we do suspect it's not all easy."

"Why do I have to be the reasonable one who cleans up after his poor planning? Again and again, people like him."

Pross held her breath for a moment, not wanting to disturb him, then held out a hand, and said, "Because you're a decent person." She considered, then added, "Also, we don't really want to let him have the fun of discovering things, do we?"

It was the last part that made Ibis relax a little. "I'm going to have to transform."

"Aren't you afraid of - I mean, if he's a snake?"

He swallowed. "That book you left, the one about hedgehogs."

"I had meant to give it to you properly." She blushed. "I suppose you found it when you were going through for the supplies list?"

He nodded. "And I was back before you were, yesterday, and I read some of it. It says that adders have a hard time biting hedgehogs. The spines, you know. Protect my nose, but that should be manageable."

Pross frowned. "Are we ... I mean, convinced about this?"

"I presume you selected a well-researched book on the topic. Being you. If you were going to give it to me."

She had to duck her head again before she laughed. "Well, best I could find on short notice. But it seemed solid enough."

"How about this? We tell the Guard - and Richart, who has friends in useful places - that we're going to try something that may be a little iffy. Can they be ready in case we need a Healer. I shift, pretend to stay in the very well-placed tent you set up, and go have a look. Once I figure out what's going on, we can make more useful plans."

Pross considered. She was quiet for a minute, then two.

Finally, she nodded. "That's as good as we're going to get, I agree."

When Richart returned, they explained their plan, such as it was. Richart wrinkled his nose, and if one knew he was also a hare, one could nearly see the ears twitching in discomfort. "I suppose needs must."

From there, it was a matter of a simple sleight of hand. Ibis retreated into the tent to review some plans and materials. The young men were directed to do things elsewhere in the site and everyone encouraged Philly to have a nice cup of tea with the Guard at the distant worktable. Richart wandered around outside, sketching things, if not nearly as well as Pross would have.

She followed Ibis into the tent. He murmured, "I promise I won't be foolish." There was that rush of him being out of focus, and then there he was. She picked him up, realising the tremendous vulnerability he must feel.

Telling her had clearly been part, but there was more. She was so much bigger than he was, as a hedgehog, and picking him up made her feel how absolute that was. And yet, there was also something deeply intimate about touching him like this, lifting him. She cupped her hand under him, then checked to make sure no one was near the tent, before she carried him to the opening they'd been working at.

The hedgehog paused at the entrance for a moment, then disappeared into the dark, and Pross now had to figure out how to avoid staring after him. She was certain staring would be a problem. Entirely too obvious.

She waited five minutes, then five more, and then she couldn't sit still any longer.

"I'm going to try to open this further, Richart." she called out. "Carefully. Do you want to help?"

Richart joined her, each of them working with trowels, pausing now and then for one of the young men to take a bucket of dirt to their tip site. When they were alone, a good half hour into the work, Richart murmured, "Are you worried?"

Pross nodded. "He's a grown man, and a sensible and skilled one, but that doesn't mean things can't go wrong."

She looked up to find Richart watching her. "I think I'd be a very different sort of man if I'd had someone care about me like that." He worked for a little more, revealing a larger opening they could clear, probably enough to fit a woman's shoulders. "You didn't talk him out of it, though?"

Pross shook her head. "I think he'd hate himself, eventually. If something happened. Even if Aimtree seems awful, he hasn't been the kind of awful who should die for it. That I know of, anyway." Richart made a strangled sound, but Pross continued. "But more to that, we really do want to see what's in there. I'd have offered to go, but he'd have refused, and anyway, his skills are more useful than mine, several ways round."

They worked in silence for a few minutes more, clearing enough of the opening she thought she could fit through, if she changed into better clothing for it. "Now, though, you're going to want to go through."

"It's been what, nearly an hour? When it's an hour, I'll go in. Let me go change."

Richart let her go without another comment, turning to finish clearing the rock. She slipped into the tent to change into a closely fitting pair of trousers and vest, and to pack up various of the items she'd gathered the day before.

THIRTY-SIX

NEAR NORWICH

I bis was not at all sure what to expect. He worried, for a minute, about light, but then realised that there was a faint glow, coming from further inside the hill. Being in this form always took him a minute to get used to. It wasn't just his senses that were different, as he'd explained to Pross. It was his feet, and how his legs moved, and how the highest point of his body wasn't his head, but the middle of his back.

He took a moment, huddled near the entrance, to get his bearings. It looked like there was a much older wall, just beyond, like they had theorised, leading into a room of some kind. Ibis took his time, listening closely, getting a sense of the space. His eyesight was poor, even with the light, giving him shifting patterns of browns and creams, not nearly as much detail as he might like.

Ibis could hear something, deeper into the opening. His choices were to investigate or go back and going back wouldn't get them more knowledge. He went forward, listening, smelling, peering for any sign of what had happened.

The first signs were the sweep of a serpentine body

across the floor, leaving tracks in the dust. It was not a big snake, as snakes go, but that was not at all reassuring. He could see, however, that the snake had not come back out this way. There was only the one track, not crossing itself. He sniffed again, getting stone and dry earth and dust, but also a hint of something dry and acrid.

It was a pity no one had written a book of what other things smelled like if you were a hedgehog. The thought almost made him laugh, and then he got hold of himself and continued.

The narrow entrance extended perhaps ten feet before opening into a larger room, with the light filtering in. It looked almost as if it had been an old bathhouse near an existing spring. Ibis could taste the damp, now, and feel the ground change a little under his claws. He kept to the side of the hallway, to attract less attention, keep in shadow. He thought back through what he knew of snakes, that the movement might attract them. If it was Aimtree, if Aimtree was a snake, he'd been in here for five or six hours now. Lack of food, lack of water, they could do odd things to a person. Especially a person who was a snake.

Edging toward the large room, Ibis realised something was queer. He could see the light, which was steady. Then he could see a long form of a snake, pressed up against a low wall, what might have been an altar, once. As he slipped into the room, the snake realised he was there, and lashed out.

Ibis retreated, then realised he was slipping into a dip in the floor, what might be a drain. He scrambled as best he could, coming to a stop balancing on some piece of it. The water below smelled of mould and damp, and he could barely peer over the top. He could see vague shapes behind the snake, what looked like sticks, but he couldn't make them out. The more he looked, the more it seemed the snake might be pinned there, somehow.

He thought about shifting, but that seemed risky. Not just in what it would confirm for Aimtree. If that was Aimtree. He was close enough that if he fell or stumbled, he might be in the snake's reach. He couldn't tell, his perspective was so different. It seemed like far enough, and yet.

Ibis summoned all his patience. Pross and Richart knew where he was. They'd work something out. Or call inside. Until they did that, he would stay where he was, it was a stable place to be.

He was beginning to regret that decision when he first heard a noise from the entrance. It felt like he'd been balancing in the drain for hours, given how his legs were aching. First, he heard a whisper of footsteps in the passage, and then saw Pross's head, appearing.

The snake lashed out impotently in her direction. She didn't quite scream, but it was a near thing, all sharp inhales and squeaks. He could see her shiver, before she drew in a breath, and stood in the entry to the room.

"Well, isn't that a curious thing?" Pross said. "You're not going anywhere, are you?" She was doing her best to be calm, and it was almost working.

She looked around, carefully, then summoned light into her hand, setting it up above her head so she could get a good view of the room. She took her time, examining each crevice, but couldn't quite venture to get to Ibis. She must have thought the snake was too close.

The snake hissed and did its best to pull away from the stone, utterly unsuccessful. She tsked and said, "As long as you stay over there. Hmm. I think I have just the thing."

Three things, it turned out. One was a small ball, something fragrant with spices and sweetness and a scent he couldn't quite identify that was like a heavy weight on his senses. It had a small wick leading from it that dangled out for an inch. She drew out a tin of matches, and set both things on the floor. Then, she brought up something that was unmistakably a gas mask.

Ibis couldn't help hissing, with an edge of something higher and sharper. The noise caught her attention, and she said, "Moment," as if she was talking to the air. "I have a plan."

He couldn't do anything but trust. She settled the gas mask over her head, testing the seal with all the attention of someone who'd needed it to survive in the War. She lit a match, then the cord, holding it upright until the entire ball started smoking. Then she bent, rolling it like a croquet ball to a point near where the snake was pinned. The snake tried to knock it away, but couldn't get the movement, the leverage, to do it.

The smoke stayed on the side of the room, and as soon as the snake stopped thrashing, she leaned over, quickly, to reach for Ibis. She set him down in the passage, murmuring "When you're ready. Mask in the bag," before she turned her full attention back to the chamber.

He took several minutes to shift, fumble for the mask, and catch his breath. When he finally joined Pross in the entrance to the chamber, he was startled to see that there was a naked man there. Aimtree, decidedly, and still pinned against the wall by some charm. Pross had lit a small brazier with a blue flame that seemed to do something. The brazier flame changed from blue to green to yellow, and it was not until it shifted to a more normal flame colour that Pross turned to him. She took off her mask, first.

"I had a very useful day yesterday. The first incense, it's a classic recipe for sleep. The brazier clears it."

"Cleverest of women." Ibis breathed it out. He wanted to hug her, to twirl around with her, and there was no time for any of that. She flushed, but she kept watching Aimtree.

"What do we do with him, then?" Which was the question. They heard a sound behind them, and Richart came through. "The young men are guarding the opening. I'm afraid they realised something was going on. Oh, goodness. I've explained to Philly we'll need a few minutes at least, she's arranging a picnic supper from the pub, it'll keep her busy."

Aimtree stirred and Pross rummaged in her bag. She came out with a piece of cloth that had likely been intended as a picnic blanket, a gaudy thing dyed in bright stripes of red and blue. "Cover yourself." She tossed the cloth at Aimtree, who reached out instinctively to catch it before he realised what it was.

Ibis had never seen another man turn quite that shade of red, all over, before. It was scientifically intriguing. Almost.

They gave Aimtree a few minutes to gather himself, and Pross poured out a cup of tea from her thermos, sliding it over to him. "Now. Why are you here?"

Ibis had not expected the amount of fear there, or the way it immediately had Aimtree babbling. "You can't tell, please, they can't find out, they'll disown me, or worse. You wouldn't, wouldn't do that to someone. Give me to the Silence, first."

It bubbled out, like lancing a boil that had been building for a lifetime. Fear of being trapped, fear of being known as a shifter, fear of discovery, fear of what they were going to do to him, that his family would disown him. It turned into a torrent of incoherence, and then into begging to be let free, they would not leave him, would they?

Pross said, very mildly, considering. "We were not the ones lashing out with fangs. You can stay pinned there until we decide what to do." She made no promises, and there was a coolness in her manner that Ibis found fascinating, even while he focused on the questions.

When Aimtree's pleas ran down, Pross said again. "Tell us what you know, and we'll see what we can do for you. Both freeing you - which may take some work - and seeing what we can do to reduce charges."

That got a "Charges?"

"For a start, trespassing. Trespassing with intent to steal a magical item, that's much more serious. Attacking me, even if it didn't do any good." Ibis noted she was leaving him out of this. "As well as whatever else you've been up to. I'm sure there's a nice long list."

Ibis realised that she had all the sharpness, the no-nonsense decision-making of a nurse in a field hospital. She was not letting anything stand between her and her goals. There was no dithering, no fussing. Just the questions and the expectation of answers.

She was getting better results than he would, too. Aimtree clearly had no idea what to do when questioned by a woman, and someone from near enough his own social class.

Pross had been picking her words carefully, Ibis realised, accentuating her accent, all the little class markers he paid such attention to, so people would see him as like them. On her, though, it gave her status, made her more like Aimtree, less like someone who wished him ill. An older aunt, verbally rapping a young man over the knuckles.

"And if I talk?"

"We'll see what we can do. I can't promise without information."

Aimtree curled himself around the cup of tea in his hand, tugging the blanket to cover more of him. It didn't improve his dignity. "Can you get me some clothes?"

"We're not sure how to get you free yet." He frowned, as if trying to decide what that meant for him. Pross continued, evenly. "If you cooperate, we'll see about getting you out of there as promptly as possible. Professor Hase here, knows a lot of useful people."

Aimtree blinked at Richart and then murmured. "Sir." He sounded very cowed now.

Richart snorted, quietly enough only they heard it, and murmured in Ibis's ear. "My reputation precedes me."

"Come on. Will you tell us?"

Aimtree nodded. "I will."

"Wait. What have you been up to?"

They were in the village where Cammie's tutoring house was, in a private room at the inn. Cammie stood, fists on her hips, glaring at her mother.

"And when were you going to tell me?"

Pross looked back, and said, as evenly as she could manage. "Now, if you'll let us." She knew this had to be a shock, on several fronts, but she wasn't sure how she could have handled it better.

Everything had snowballed from that initial night in his flat to the discoveries, to a long day spent figuring out how to release the magical traps. It had taken a day to talk to the Guard, and several more securing the site. Only then had she managed more than a brief note to her daughter, and the bare brief pause for May Day morning in True Eyeworth and the necessary rituals.

"Us?" The pitch of Cammie's voice rose.

Ibis murmured, "Let me see about some food and drinks."

Pross nodded at him, grateful he made the offer. Cammie kept glowering at her.

Once Ibis was gone, Pross let out a breath, and said, "Look. I'm sorry. I messed up."

That, at least, was novel enough that Cammie blinked. "Mum, you're always right. Always but always."

That made Pross laugh. "No, love, I'm not. I just do my best to make it seem that way."

It broke the tension. Not all of it, but enough that Cammie took a step back, and leaned back on the sturdy table against the wall. "Where'd he go then?"

"To get some food."

"He didn't ask what I wanted." There was the pouting again.

"No, love. I except he'll ask them what you like. You're in here often enough, I told him that when I told him we'd meet here."

"Not at the house?"

Pross shook her head. "It's the kind of talk wants a bit of privacy."

"Are you going to marry him?" And then there was the glorious early teenage dawning horror. "Or do things with him? Where I can see?"

Pross was amused. All right, they could get somewhere useful from here. "We're talking about what things might look like, long-term. But not marriage, not yet. And only if you decide you don't mind him too much. At least as long as you're in school. You're my daughter, love, and you come first. He understands that."

Cammie looked dubious, and more than a bit rebellious, but she finally grunted. "I'm not giving up my room."

"I wouldn't expect that, no." Besides the fact that if they

were living together, she wanted Ibis firmly in her own bed, thank you.

There was a long pause, Cammie clearly trying to decide what to ask first. Pross moved to sit down in one of the more comfortable chairs. "When did it happen? I mean, whatever ... changed."

Pross considered, and then said "Beginning of the month, both of us realising ... we'd like to try more things."

"In Paris?" Cammie clearly thought Paris had a lot to answer for.

"I kissed him in Paris. And then we went our separate ways and thought about what we wanted. Trying to be reasonable about it."

"And?" Cammie seemed almost unbelieving.

"I spent the night at his flat, that Saturday, after we'd been to Schola to consult one of his old professors."

Cammie pushed away from the table, to pace. Pross watched her, and felt the ache of her like her father she could be, the length of the stride, the forcefulness. "What house was he?"

"Seal. We were consulting the Master of the House, Professor Hase."

"About what?"

"The archaeology. Finding the lost hoard. Which we've found, mind you, but that's what took me all week to sort out. We've been taking shifts sleeping on site to make sure it was safe until we got proper protections up."

"I should be angry with you."

"I should have told you sooner, poppet, but it just all came on in a rush, the last few weeks."

"Are you going to tell me now? About the dig?"

"Of course. That's part of why we're here."

Cammie made another pass around the room, not quite

hitting the corner of the table, then she whirled around. "Tell him he can come in. If he's got cakes."

Pross laughed and said. "Will." before she opened the door. Ibis had a table near the other side, with a tray. A small tower of cakes and sandwiches, a pot of tea and a bottle of lemonade. He looked up, inquiringly.

"She's angry at me, but you can come in. If you have cakes, she said, but you're ahead of me there."

"I asked what she liked, and they were glad to help." Ibis smiled slightly, then sobered. "She has more than enough reason." Ibis was quiet, but Pross nodded in return. He was right. And she'd known Cammie would be upset. This way, though, they could at least get it all over with at once. She held the door, and Ibis brought the tray in, setting it down.

Cammie made her way over, stalking as only a thirteen-year-old could, and eyed the offerings, before turning to face him, her curls bouncing. "You're not completely awful."

Pross snorted, and said, "So, about the archaeology. The last I wrote, we were going out to the site to see what we could find. It got a lot more interesting from there. Part way through that first day, we suspected someone had got into the hoard. We were right - we got in, and found someone had snuck in, using a particular kind of magic, and got stuck to one of the traps."

"What kind of magic?"

"We promised we wouldn't tell, if he behaves." Pross said, watching Cammie closely. Her daughter was clearly not pleased with that decision.

Ibis picked up. "But then we had to figure out what to do with him. Which was complicated."

Cammie frowned. "Why was it complicated?"

"Some of it is that he's a silly man." Pross thought about

how to say this. She'd been thinking about it since they caught him. "It turns out he'd been working with a bunch of people who wanted to hoard all the things in the Research Society. Not do much work, not share what they knew, but laze around and do things they wanted, that helped them."

This was enough of a puzzle that Cammie finally sat down, reaching for one of the chocolate cakes. "Why was he silly?"

"He's the sort of man who always had things given to him. White, from one of the First Families, lots of money." Pross was trying to figure out how to explain it.

"Some people - men, especially - feel like everything is theirs. Unless they feel like sharing, because they can't be bothered with whatever it is."

Cammie was quiet for a good thirty seconds. "How do I know you're not like that?" She looked up at Ibis, very determined.

Ibis paused, setting his hands. "Well, first, that lot wouldn't have me. As they proved. I'm not from that sort of family. And I've been in plenty of places where people wanted to take things from me. I know what it's like, and I try not to do it to other people."

Cammie cocked her head, considering. "What do you do when they try to take things?"

"Mostly," Ibis glanced for a moment at Pross. "Mostly, I try to be smarter than they are. If I have to I'll fight, or figure out how to get things done. That's why I kept helping your mother. Even when people made it clear that I should stop."

That earned him a long thoughtful look, then a, "Mum?"

"I think he likes a bit of a challenge, personally." Pross said, more easily, hoping this might work, all of it. "But he is really very smart. And he knows different languages than I do, which is handy. And a lot of other things."

"Which ones?"

Ibis took a breath. "There's something I haven't told your mother yet."

"Your afternoon appointment?" Pross had, of course, been curious. But she also assumed he had a reason for waiting to tell her.

Ibis nodded. "We had the help of Professor Hase, who is the head of Seal House. He told me that they're looking to hire one or two new people for next year. Teaching Arabic - I'm fluent in that. Or possibly in Materia, focusing on evaluating materials and the theory behind different materials."

Cammie frowned. "So you'd be at Schola when I was?"

"My youngest sister will be in her last year, next year. So I need to talk it through with her. You wouldn't have to take classes with me, there are ways to avoid that."

Cammie frowned, then said, distracted, "The Arabic sounds sort of interesting."

"I could teach you separately, if you wanted. Your mother might want to learn it too."

Pross murmured, "Thanks, I would." Her daughter could be lured with languages, rather like Octavian had.

"Where would you live?"

"Probably in one of the cottages."

"And Mum?"

"Your mum has only just heard about this." Pross pointed out. "But we could work something out. If nothing else, I'm sure Geoffrey will let us make arrangements for regular use of the portal."

"I'd not ask your mother to move without something for her in it. Being a housewife is a fine thing, but that'd be wasting a lot of her skills. Richart - Professor Hase - thought the bookseller in the village might want to sell on the business in a couple of years. He doesn't have an apprentice to take over easily." He offered this to Pross as a tentative fragile gift.

She smiled at him. "So. We can talk about all of that. We haven't told you the rest about our dissolute young man."

Cammie tilted her head. "Is he in a lot of trouble?"

"A lot, but less than he might be if he hadn't told us what he did. Mind, there he was, pinned to a wall in the middle of a sort of dank Roman building. All covered over with earth, with no help of getting out if we didn't figure out how to free him. It made him a lot more willing to talk."

"He really didn't have a lot of dignity," Ibis agreed, managing not to laugh at the memory.

Pross grinned at him. "He really didn't. So we let him squirm, just a little. Then we gave him some tea and something to eat. And then we got him talking enough that we knew who should be told in the Guard."

"Why did you have to think about that? Couldn't you just, report it? You always told me to find the Guard if I had a problem."

"It was a delicate sort of problem, and some powerful people. So we needed to make sure that they didn't just toss the dissolute young man aside and get out of trouble. The good thing about Professor Hase being on our side is that he knew a lot of the right people to talk to. He'd taught a lot of them, or sometimes their parents. He helped us get the right people listening, so we could fix things. Or get started on it."

Cammie considered, then said, "And is it fixed?"

"It'll take more work, but there are senior people in the Research Society sorting that bit out, so we can focus on the dig. You can come help when you're out for the summer. We'll be there for a while yet."

"What if I don't want to dig in the dirt?"

"Then we'll figure something else out. But the research part of the hoard is really interesting. We could use someone to help us keep the notes in order and help me do sketches of what we're finding."

Cammie seemed unconvinced. But she fell so easily into a discussion of what archaeology involved, and what use she might be, that Pross had reason to hope this might just work out.

THIRTY-EIGHT

TRUE EYEWORTH

P ross stretched out on her bed, then shifted onto one elbow, watching Ibis. They had retreated to her flat above the bookstore, for privacy and because she had the larger bed.

She'd undressed enough to slip into a loose robe, but they'd not got further than that. Yet. Mind, the line of her leg under the robe was exceedingly tempting.

"Two things," she said, after a moment.

"The offer?" Ibis felt sheepish.

Pross laughed at his expression, then relented. "You have a rummage in the drawer there, see if there's anything you find interesting."

He blinked, then rolled over, stretching to reach for the bedside table. He pulled the drawer open, and held up a smooth curved wooden object, perhaps six inches long, that tapered and swelled. "Madam enjoys devices, then?" He recognised the overall idea of the thing, to slip inside her, and the knob on the end suggested other actions.

"Madam did not have a lot of other options for a few years." It came out with a half-laugh, then she murmured,

"It wasn't just my heart missing Octavian. My body did, too. I felt so hollow for a long time."

Ibis bent to kiss her, tenderly, before he moved to pull her small collection where he could investigate them. The fact she'd pointed them out made her plans for the rest of their evening rather clear.

"The offer," Pross said. "Are you going to take it?"

"Unless you don't want me to, yes. I think..." He had to set the wooden toy in his hand down, to find the words. "I assume that the Society will get sorted out, but I admit I'm bitter about it. I don't much enjoy cleaning up other people's messes."

Pross cocked her head, considering. "You've done enough of that for a lifetime."

"More than enough. And ..." He shook his head. "Aimtree wasn't even an interesting ass. Just your garden variety child of privilege and power, who had no interest in anything other than his own pleasures."

"Stubborn as an ass, too." Poss said. "He was terrified, though. That we knew he could shift." She paused and said, "Not that I didn't believe you, about them - using people who could. But the way he was." She shivered.

Ibis reached out a hand to rest on her leg again. "He's right that they might disown him for it. Some people would. Because of the superstitions around it. And he's right the risk, even now, that he'd get sent to some foreign dangerous place."

Pross frowned. "Would they?"

"Probably. I don't know if he hates everywhere that isn't England, or is terrified of it, or both. But I think it would destroy him. Richart and I are sure now that his uncle pulled a lot of strings to keep him in England, during the War."

"Why did he learn to shift, if he was afraid?"

"I suspect he thought, when he was younger and even more foolish, that it would give him power. Or let him get things. He's not that big as a snake, he could easily hide in a room, under something, and overhear quite a lot. Blackmail's a powerful motivation."

"Is that why people hate shifters? That particular fear?"

Ibis's tone was dry. "It doesn't help. But I think it's more - some people are terrified by things they can't do. Or things they can't imagine doing. Or things they can't control. If you add it all up, there's a lot of fear there."

Pross frowned, shook herself, then changed the subject. "Do you think you'd like teaching?"

"From what Richart said, maybe. I'd be a lot more nervous, going into it without him to tell me how things work. There's a number of older professors retiring in the next few years, a chance to shape how things go."

"Materia? Or Arabic?" Her voice had turned curious.

"I think the materia. I'm not primarily a maker, but apparently they want someone to do more of the theory. Possibly some simpler creation work, but I know a fair bit of that from Ummi and her charms and talismans."

"I think you should take it, if you want to. We'll work the rest out."

Ibis beamed down at her, startled. "I thought you'd take longer to decide." He'd expected a lot longer.

That earned him a twitch of her shoulder, in amusement. "You make me impulsive, haven't we proved that already? But it feels right. And you could be happy there. Not just - existing."

"You're very generous." Ibis teased her, then let his fingers drop to trace the line of her hip, suggesting other forms of generous enjoyment.

"Oh, you can do something in return." She was laughing now, complete at ease, like all the tension of the day had just popped.

"What do these devices do, then?" He could take the hint.

She waved a hand. "The one with the blue end pulses. The green one vibrates. The one with the gold crystal, it..." She arched her back, entirely instinctively. "It feels like everything's wonderful."

It made his decision easy, at least to start with. "Oh, I know what we're doing, then."

He wanted her, in so many ways. The way she stretched out now, watching him, her eyes half-lidded. He loved how she was so utterly secure in herself, so much of the time, and yet he could surprise her. He wanted a lifetime of earning that quick sharp smile of startled delight from her. A lifetime of bringing her pleasure. And so many conversations about books and museums and fabulous travels they hadn't had yet.

That could wait. Now, he reached to help her slip the robe off, tossing it off the side of the bed with grand abandon. Ibis ran his hands along her body, skin against skin, tracing and feeling the shape of her, the dips and curves. He loved this, how she reacted to his touch, like a cat wanting more. When she was like this, she was utterly free, all impulse and desire. Hathor's daughter, truly.

She stretched a little before meeting his eyes. "And what are you going to do, then?"

"Patience, you." Ibis was grinning now. "I'm not telling. You lie back and enjoy."

Pross laughed, then wriggled, to centre herself on the bed. "You know you want me." Her hand shifted, and he arched, feeling her fingers run along his cock.

"Not arguing that. Your pleasure first, lady who glad-dens my heart."

It was the endearment that did it, he suspected. Seeing how it made her gasp, and then her legs parted a little more for him, something utterly instinctive and willing. He let his fingers slip between her legs, touching and stroking. He wanted her damp and ready, reaching for it, before he used her toy.

Touches turned into shivers, murmurs into moans. Once she was quivering and needy, he finally relented. He pressed the base of the toy, felt it warm in his hand, like a glow for the soul, then set the head of the device against her opening. Ibis shifted the angle, slipping it in.

She arched, almost immediately, like she'd wanted something to clench herself around. He grunted, realising what it would be like when he entered her, and her hand grabbed at his arm. "More, please, oh, more." The neediness in her voice nearly broke him, made him want to cover her with his body and bury himself inside her, but no. Not yet.

He moved the toy, and then felt it slip in, then deeper, to fill her. Her hips bucked, and now she was panting, utterly frantic with pleasure. He found, to his delight, that it did not quite tip her over into a climax, not without some other stimulation. Instead the toy kept her in a place where she was overwhelmed with a visible ecstasy.

Ibis stretched out along her side, nipping and nuzzling at her ear, her neck. His hand worked the toy in a steady rhythm between her legs that matched the roll of his cock against her hip.

Her voice was a low chant of "Oh, oh, oh please, more, yes." Something in him was exultant. He could do this for eternity, be lost in the endless waves of touch and intimacy, giving her pleasure. Finding his in pleasing her, in her responses.

After some time, his hand ached, and his cock ached even more, throbbing with his pulse. Finally, he drew back from her, moving, even though she cried out and clutched wordlessly at his hand.

He bent to kiss her as he rearranged, held steady through her nails sharply pressing against his arm as he withdrew the toy. Then, with no pause at all, he found her entrance, and slid in. All the way in, one deep, needy thrust. It had him throwing his head back and groaning. He heard her voice join his, a higher counterpoint of breathy, "Yes, oh, more, love."

They were frantic, then, all thrusting and clenching and tangled in each other. He fed from her responses, and she fed from his. Her legs came up around his waist to tighten and hold him close, until he was driving in and out in rapid sharp thrusts, building and building.

Finally, he shifted, to the angle he'd learned brought her the greatest pleasure, thrust twice, and felt her explode. The way she tightened around him, around his cock, made him grunt. He thrust and pressed, and sucked at her neck, until he felt her shudders finally slow, before he joyously could follow her. He poured himself out into her, body and soul, needy at first, then finally easing to rock against her, an arm drawing her closer as he slipped to the side.

They lay there, drifting and breathing, for what seemed like an eternity. He felt her hand slip into his, and the delighted whisper in his ear, "Keeping you."

EPILOGUE

SCHOLA

The door of the cottage opened, then closed. Ibis poked his head out of the little kitchen area. "How did it go?"

Pross held up her hand, then shrugged out of her coat, stretching. The dress she was wearing was beautiful, and well-tailored, but it felt like armour. "Let me change, all right?" She'd been here twice, so far, since Ibis had moved in. It was enough to know where things were, but it didn't quite feel like home for either of them yet.

She ducked into the small bedroom, making short work of putting on a looser and much more comfortable house dress, before she came back out.

Ibis was just bringing a tray out to the table in front of the fire, and he held up a bottle.

"We have something to drink to, yes." She set her satchel on the floor, by her chair. "I think we'll be able to come to terms. He wasn't sure, at first. I mean, I don't have his credentials as a scholar, or his long experience. There are clearly reasons no one else has wanted to take it on."

"But?"

"I asked him about some of the questions he's helped with, the materials he's tracked down for people. He was..." She frowned. "He was dismissive, at first. But he mentioned something about a project in Hungary, and I talked about visiting there with Octavian."

Ibis cocked his head. "And?"

She smiled. "We've agreed to have me try a handful of cases with him. He'll pay me, and I can draw on his resources, but he wants to see how I go about doing them. The good news is it will be good reason to be here at least for a long weekend every month, to check in with him."

"I believe I can keep my schedule as free as possible." Ibis offered a glass of wine to her. "To your successful research."

Pross laughed and tapped her glass to his. "May it be so." she agreed.

"And your bookshop?"

"I'll work on training someone in. I've had a couple of inquiries about taking an apprentice, from people who'd like to be in the area, so I..." She rubbed her face. "I suppose it's time to interview the two I know about. See if there's anyone else." She looked at him, searching. "It'll be a couple of years, before ... before I can move."

"You come here. More than once a month if you've an apprentice to mind the place. I'll come there on vacations. We have the portal."

"I'm working on talking Carillon into supporting one in the village. We really should have one. I agree with his concerns about security, for Ytene."

"Is he coming around?" Ibis was dubious about Carillon still. They'd been circling each other slowly.

Pross snorted. "Well, Lizzie's on my side, so we're quite sure he will soon."

It was then they heard the sound of voices, coming closer, down the road, and Ibis said, "Let me get that, you've had quite the walk today."

She shook her head. "I'd like to see my daughter's doing well, ta." So they opened the door together, watching Hypatia and Cammie coming down the lane toward the cottage. They were chattering away, easily, not the stilted conversation of being polite to each other.

When Cammie saw her, though, she broke off, and came running, flinging herself into Pross's arms. "Mum! It's wonderful! And I'm learning so much, and there's so many assignments, and how did you ever manage it, but it's grand, and thank you for making me learn my Latin properly, you have no idea how much it's helping."

Pross laughed, loudly. "I'm glad you're settling in, and yes, it's a lot of work, but that's your job right now, learning all the things and then some. And I had an idea about the Latin, that's why I made you learn it right the first time."

Cammie took a step back and then ducked her head. "Um. Professor Ward?" She clearly wasn't sure how to address him, it was the first time she'd been to the cottage.

"We really should decide what you want to call me when we're being family."

"Ibis," Hypatia slipped into give him a hug, and he hugged her back. "Cammie, Arabic's got a ton of words for relationships."

"For now, Ibis is fine, if you'd like. Or if you think of something else, you can ask."

Cammie nodded, a little shy, and Pross tapped her shoulder. "We have cake and chai and - well, the adults have wine."

"Does that mean it went well, mum?"

"Nothing settled yet, but I'm in with a good chance.

And it means I'll need to be here regularly for a while, so you can tell me all about what you're up to and get a lunch out."

"Oh, Merlin's knights and all their adventures, the food is odd. And the dorms, sleeping with other people right there, how do you do it? Two of them snore." Cammie was bubbling over again, and Pross nudged her inside, letting her talk.

She felt Ibis lean in, his hand on her back. "We'll be grand, my lady. Grand and glorious."

IF YOU ENJOYED *Magician's Hoard* and would like to read more of this series, please sign up for my mailing list to get all the latest news and fun extras. Your reviews (on whatever review site you use) are much appreciated, too!

As a thank you, you'll get a prequel novella, *Ancient Trust*, that shares more about Lord Geoffrey Carillon's inheritance of the land magic in 1922. It mentions a number of events around True Eyeworth.

Read on for more historical details about this book and an excerpt from *Wards of the Roses*.

AUTHOR'S NOTES

This was such a delightful book to write! The 1920s are a particularly rich period for Egyptology (even if some of it rather misguided).

Before we go any further, I want to thank Kiya Nicoll for the Egyptological consultation on this one, as well as being the best editor I could ever hope for. (Other services have included taming my commas, telling me when I need more ponies, and helping me sort out plot complexities. As well as telling me when I need to add another chapter.)

The Petrie collection of the time is much as Ibis describes it: William Matthew Flinders Petrie was still actively excavating in Egypt through around 1933. I had a chance to go to a lecture there in 2015 (on the Egyptology in the Classic *Doctor Who* episode *Pyramids of Mars* because I am entirely that sort of geek.) It's an amazing teaching collection with stunningly important historical objects every time you turn around. If you're at all interested in Egypt's vast history, I recommend the Petrie Museum website and museum to you.

The **Professor Murray** Ibis mentions in passing is Dr Margaret Murray, known as a quite accomplished archaeologist and Egyptologist, but better known these days for rather less historically rigorous ideas about European witchcraft.

I loved having the chance in this book to show the kinds of religious practices that might have carried through in the magical community from ancient Egypt. Ibis is particularly devoted to **Djehuty** (more commonly known in English as Thoth). Commonly depicted with an ibis head (for the similarity to a scribe's pen), he was also associated with the baboon, hence the items in Ibis's office.

Hetheru, also known as Hathor, was traditionally depicted with the head of a cow, and Ibis makes reference to her horns. She was associated with lovemaking, beauty, music, dancing, and joy. The line Ibis recites in chapter 26 comes from one of the prayers to her found in a papyrus from the Middle Kingdom period.

Rudyard Kipling was still alive and actively writing in this period - more than once I had to go and double check that something I wanted to refer to had been published already! As Pross says, he can go from amazing to agonising in a matter of a sentence or two, if you're aware of the underlying politics of empire and India in particular.

Acting Brigadier-General Reginald Dyer was in command of British Indian Army troops who shot into a crowd of Punjabi men, women, and children gathered in peaceful protest in April 1919. The troops ended up killing nearly 400 people in a crowd of 1,500 during what became known as the Jallianwala Bagh or Amritsar Massacre.

Michael O'Dwyer was the Lieutenant-Governor of

Punjab at the time. He had approved Dyer's actions and many believe him to have been the main planner. (O'Dwyer was killed by an activist who had been wounded in the massacre in 1940.)

Finally, there are so many variants of **shape-shifting**, and in the world of the Mysterious Charm, there is no need to pick just one. I knew Ibis was a shifter (and into a hedgehog) from fairly early on, but I wanted to write about a magical ability that is often associated with curses, wrongdoing, and stigma in many mediaeval and other historical texts. However, Ibis is the most adorable hedgehog, and hedgehogs are found both in England and in Egypt.

The appearance of a snake cult half way through the book surprised me (and I suspect they still may be up to things in the larger world, despite being foiled here...). And the sirrush is a fascinating creature, also known as a mušḫuššu. You can, however, see why I went for sirrush for the book... But there you are. Sometimes a novel needs a snake cult.

(If you'd like to see more about the aftermath of the snake cult, *Point By Point* picks up that thread of the story.)

I hope you'll join me for book four, *Wards of the Roses*, about a manor mysteriously reappearing in the Oxfordshire countryside after several hundred years. (It takes place in 1922, and explains how Captain Lefton, introduced at the end of *Outcrossing*, got her job.)

My authorial wiki (bit.ly/celia-lake-wiki) has pages, timelines, and maps that connect characters, places, and events in various ways. Please let me know if there's additional information that would be helpful to you.

The newsletter (https://www.celialake.com/news letter/) and my social media accounts will have all the details about new and upcoming releases, and I hope to see you one of those places! Until then, happiest of reading to you.

As always, reviews and comments on the books are always welcome!